CONTE

MW00933883

Preface

Are there specific incidents in your youth that you cannot get out of your head? The author repeatedly played his memories in his mind and knew there would come a day when he would write down those happenings.

These short stories are not unique. The reader has many similar memories, such as those herein. Relate them to family and friends. Write them down! Don't let the memories be forgotten. That is the main objective of *"The Wind is Forever."*

Enjoy!

TODD

The day was lovely! On such a day, an ordinary boy would be restless confined indoors.

Other than having two mothers, Todd was the typical American boy. His hair was so blond and cropped so short it appeared white. He was ten years old and in Mr. Sánchez's fifth-grade classroom. Todd was stout, yet it enhanced his appearance; it gave him a healthy look.

Mr. Sánchez sensed the anxiousness of the students, particularly the boys. They longed to play baseball outside while the swings and jump ropes beckoned the girls.

The teacher resolved to do something about this discontent. Mr. Sánchez asked the students to put away all materials, close their eyes, and rest their heads on their desks.

He commenced relating a story that perfectly fits the situation everyone was feeling on this gorgeous day.

Mr. Sánchez meandered between the rows of desks as he relayed his story. He noticed Todd no longer rested his head on his desk; instead, he wrote in his notebook while the teacher narrated.

Mr. Sánchez held a very soft spot for Todd as he consoled the well-mannered, friendly boy through the ribbing others handed out while Todd was outside the classroom. Todd didn't know his biological father. His mom had been in a relationship with another lady since he was an infant. Some boys gave Todd a hard time about his "two mothers." That home situation made Todd a good target for unfeeling children choosing to have fun at someone else's expense.

(Boys can be both: the kindest or the cruelest.)

Todd was highly well-adjusted, especially for his age, but still, a new boy or boys from another class amused themselves by making fun of Todd.

Mr. Sánchez, at first, condoned Todd's actions. He continued his story and his movement around the classroom.

Mr. Sánchez's tenderness for Todd allowed him to give Todd more leeway than customary. (Perhaps Todd was noting an essential reminder for himself.)

However, Todd's persistent writing eventually reached Mr. Sánchez's patience limit. He was pressed to stop Todd's action lest the class accuse Todd of being the *'teacher's pet.'*

With a heavy heart, Mr. Sánchez stopped right in front of Todd and asked, "Todd, is what you are writing more important than the story I am telling you?"

Everyone's heads came up! Todd's face turned tomato red as he sheepishly answered, "I tell my mothers every story you tell us, and they love them, but sometimes I forget important parts. I took notes as you taught us so I could do a better job."

Oh, no! Mr. Sánchez's face burned pink! (Why had he not shown trust enough in Todd to ignore his writing? Mr. Sánchez should have known better since Todd had never given him grief!)

Mr. Sánchez placed his right hand on Todd's shoulder (*against school policy*), asked Todd to stand up, and, with eyes watering, gave him a firm hug. The students, knowing the *teachers-don't-touch-students* rule, gasped!

Next, Mr. Sánchez apologized and asked for Todd's forgiveness.

No one ever picked on Todd again, and if a newcomer dared make fun of him, classmates were quick to defend him.

Years later, Mr. Sánchez, inspired by Todd, wrote down his stories.

THE WIND IS FOREVER

Growing up in the rural west side of the Central Valley in California, I had the most loyal friend I had ever enjoyed. Johnny was my Italian pal's name. And, though I was four years older than him and Mexican, we hit it off right away. We were about the same size and weight. One thing that made Johnny so special was he saw the heart in people, not the color of their skin.

We both loved sports, school, and good grades. Everything we did, we did with gusto—giving one hundred percent.

Spring came early in 1958, carrying a new, different feeling for Johnny. Despite the fact Johnny was only ten, he fell in love.

Sofie was her name, and she was as eye-pleasing as the spring's flowers. Sofie's perfectly symmetrical face and olive complexion added to her cuteness. If you can imagine Tony

Curtis at age ten, you have a near-perfect description of Johnny. Thus, Sofie, the sweet Mexican maiden, and Johnny, the charming Italian lad, fell head-over-heels for each other.

The handsome pair lived seven miles apart, but school brought them together. A school rule forbids *'holding hands,'* yet that did not stop Johnny and Sofie. The front office gave the word not to enforce this rule when it came to Johnny and Sofie.

The administration called it *"puppy love"* and believed it would quickly pass. {Johnny and Sofie's infatuation seemed so perfect, school administration thought it *'cute'*; and, if I did not know any better, I would say they encouraged it—it looked so pure, so innocent. Perhaps the love Johnny and Sofie's had, they wished for themselves. On the other hand, did the school pride itself in having its own "***Romeo & Juliette***?"}

Dozens of trees sprinkled the school ground; Johnny and Sofie picked the youngest, most excellent cottonwood tree. The attractive tree provided shade for a perfect patch of lawn. Even this duet—tree/lawn--appeared delighted to share what they offered with Johnny and Sofie.

In no time, Johnny and Sofie were the darlings of the six hundred or so students enrolled at this small, K-8 country school. Cantua Creek Elementary school was a jewel surrounded by fields teeming with crops. It was only five years old, and its beautiful red-brick fronts and all-glass backs added to its attractiveness.

Now, the only time I had with Johnny was at home. We lived less than two hundred yards apart in the Three Rocks village. (Johnny lived in the only decent home in the otherwise shantytown. Johnny's dad owned the Café, the bar, the gas station, and the grocery store.) That was fine with me because Johnny's friendship never wavered. After completing our school work, we practiced whatever sport our school was competing against other schools.

Soon, the school administration realized it had mistakenly allowed Johnny and Sofie to hold hands. What they thought to be a day-or-two thing had become permanent. Johnny and Sofie were sprawled under their tree holding hands and talking for every recess and lunch period.

The office called in the *"love birds"* and let them know they could hold hands no more. {Again, was the administration following the ***"Romeo & Juliette"*** script? Johnny and Sofie obeyed that rule, but it did not stop them from meeting and talking under their favorite tree.

Then came a day when Sofie was not on her bus when it arrived.

Frantic, Johnny asked other passengers about Sofie. Everyone he asked said the same thing: neither Sofie nor her two older brothers had boarded the bus. Johnny had a dreadful feeling.

It did not take long to find out Sofie's family had moved twenty miles away.

Johnny's heartache crushed his spirit. Hoping against hope, he still went to *'their'* tree every recess and lunch hour. Soon the entire school was in mourning, for everyone loved Johnny.

Having never experienced anything like this before, I was little comfort to Johnny. I could not find the right words to say to him. All I could do was be with him and share his pain.

Johnny would not eat, do his homework, or play games. Day after day, Johnny would sit at the table where we usually did our homework, his mind twenty miles away.

One day Johnny's mom came in and, in desperation, informed him he needed to apply himself to his studies, or he might fail the fifth grade. All three of us knew that was impossible, for Johnny had been an excellent student until the day Sofie moved, and the end of the school year was just around the corner.

Johnny's mom then tried a different approach. She spoke consolingly and assured Johnny that other cute girls would come along. She said, "Love is like the wind; it comes and goes."

Johnny's answer was, "Mom, you don't understand! Sofie and I love each other. We promised each other our love was forever. In our case, our love is forever just as the wind is forever."

The years passed, and I lost track of Johnny. One day word came declaring Johnny had died, and rumor had it drugs and drinking were the cause of such an early tragedy.

I did not believe it for a minute. I knew the cause of Johnny's passing. Johnny had died of a broken heart, for his love of Sofie was forever, just like the wind is forever.

El　　　　　　　　　　　Sol

Ace of the Diamond

The sun descended beyond the hills on the west side, throwing the baseball diamond into total shadow.

Yet, there was no mistake; a game had been played on this all-dirt ball field. The lime-lined markings were half gone; the batters' boxes had disappeared. Not a square foot could be found with no cleat marks.

The villages of _Agua Dulce_ (Sweetwater) and _Palos Verdes_ (Green Trees) play this game every year on September 16. A mere eight kilometers (five miles) separate these baseball-crazy villages, making for a perfect rivalry.

This year, _Tito Torres_, the "Ace of the Diamond," took the mound for the last time. Perhaps it was time, for he was forty-two and had started every game for the last twenty-five years for _Agua Dulce_.

His fastball (_béisbol fans_ called it '_bola de humo_' "smoke ball") had lost some of its hop, yet Ace more than made up for it with his curveball, screwball, and drop.

His years of experience made him a cunning, bold pitcher, thus the 'Ace of the Diamond.'

Palos Verdes had an answer for Ace: *Mando Martínez*. At eighteen the year before, he had produced the winning run with a two-run blast in the bottom of the ninth.

Mando was bigger, stronger, and faster this year, with even more power than a year ago.

Mando Martínez belonged to the rarest breed in baseball, the five-tool player.

Baseball scouts from the Mexican League and the Major Leagues had hounded him all summer. *Mando* refused to let his village down. He would sign after this game.

CRACK! CRACK! CRACK! *Mando* homered in the first, again in the fourth, and he would have homered a third time in the seventh had he not failed to touch them all in his haste to make it three consecutive homers.

At this point, Ace agreed: "This young fellow is Major League material! Perhaps God has looked down at Mexico and declared, *'The time is right for Mexico to have its own **Babe Ruth.***' There is no doubt about it; *Armando Martínez* is a NATURAL!"

Ace was grateful his team had given him three runs to back his masterful pitching. Yet, he was rightly concerned that he would have to face *Mando* in the ninth if any batter got on base.

So far, only *Mando* had gotten on base, twice with homers, and that third time when he was called out for missing third base. Ace had not walked a batter. (He loathed base-on-balls. He averaged less than one per game.) His team had yet to make an error.

For the last few innings, Ace sat away from his teammates. He did not want his mind distracted. All alone, Ace plotted how he would pitch to *Mando* if he did come to bat one more time. Ace took the mound for the ninth, hoping for three up and three down.

Alas, an error let him down. The error allowed the batter to make it safely to second base.

Ace's infielders and catcher promptly gathered at the mound to suggest the obvious and give an intentional walk to *Mando*. Doggedly, Ace shook his head, N0! His pride would not accept that. He WOULD PITCH to *Mando*! Besides, Ace would be breaking a cardinal baseball rule: Do not INTENTIONALLY put on base the WINNING run!

Agua Dulce's fans, seated on the western hills, groaned. A delighted cheer came from the eastern hills, where the *Palos Verdes* supporters were now standing.

Now, both groups stood to watch what baseball is all about: *Mano-a-mano,* batter versus pitcher, the former intently watching and waiting for the tiniest detection that would give him the edge, the latter cautiously wanting to throw off the timing of his foe. OH! How they loved this game of *béisbol!* Ace had seen enough of *Mando* to stay away from the heart of the plate. Also, he would use his fastball only as a waste pitch. That left Ace with his curveball, screwball, and drop. These pitches he had to spot these on the corners of the plate. He dared use only the black inside of home plate and the outside black border of the plate.

Ace could use three different heights: high, middle, and low. He had to avoid the central area, facilitating *Mando's* effort to get the bat's barrel on the ball. He desperately did not want that to happen.

In a nutshell, Ace had cut his nine pitching zones to four.

Mando, on the other hand, had been born to play *béisbol*. He was blessed to be a five-tool player.

Mando did not want to think about what was on the line. He needed to focus on getting the barrel of his bat on the ball. *Mando* knew Ace but admitted Ace knew him.

They had faced each other fifteen times before. *Mando* remembered the five times Ace got him out with breaking balls on the black outside of home plate.

Ace had overwhelmed *Mando* in *Mando's* first year in the league at age 15, striking him out all three times he faced him.

Mando struck out once, walked once, and hit a double and a single the following year.

When *Mando* was seventeen, he hit two homers, got nicked by a pitch, and struck out.

 Last year, Mando owned Ace, hitting a double, triple, and two homers, the last being a walk-off game-winner.

After Ace struck him out the last time two years ago, *Mando* vowed Ace would never again strike him out. *Mando* had kept to his promise, for in his last seven at-bats, he had four homers--five if you count the one where he missed a base--, a double, and a triple.

Mando Martínez stepped in; the battle was on!

Ace used only the plate's black and moved the ball up and down, inside and outside, always trying to outguess *Mando*.

Mando was on every pitch, sending missile after missile, FOUL!

Thirteen pitches later, Ace still needed one strike to get by *Mando*. And *Mando* was just as determined not to strike out. The count had been full for what seemed like hours ago. *Mando* refused to accept a walk, and Ace was unwilling to give one. *Mando* well knew he was his village's only hope.

The fans witnessed a classic confrontation of two stars, one on the way up and the other on the way out.

Throughout this whole at-bat, the fans sensed something in their heart changing. They knew both players would be winners; there would be no loser, no matter the outcome. Ace of the Diamond and *Armando Martínez* had endeared themselves to this crowd.

Adrenalin in both was flowing freely. Ace, for his part, had forgotten he was tired. *Mando,* in just this at-bat, had grown to be a man. No one noticed the sun was going down.

For his 14th pitch, Ace resolved to let the base runner take third. Ace wanted to use his windup. It gave his fastball just a tad more *"oomph."*

He scanned the fans on both hills, turned, and, in order, glanced at each of his fielders for a second or two as if acknowledging and thanking each one for years of having his back.

Perhaps the scan of the fans meant the same thing.

Ace slowly turned and climbed back on the mound.

Once on the rubber, he began to rock his body back and forth, arms swinging at his sides, allowing the runner to advance to third base.

Ace smoothly pivoted the left side of his body forward on his third rocking of the arms. With the ball in his right hand, Ace exploded forward!

Ace's best fastball of the day split the plate perfectly. Ace's selection and placement caused *Mando* to swing just the slightest fraction LATE!

Mando Martínez struck out on a pitch RIGHT DOWN THE CENTER OF THE PLATE!

With the bat still in his left hand, *Mando* glared at Ace; then came a slight smile, and with his right hand, *Mando Martínez* tipped his cap out of respect, and Ace of the Diamond returned the gesture.

The *béisbol*-loving fans from *Agua Dulce* and *Palos Verdes* came out of their daze and began a prolonged cheer, which echoed through the hills.

The *béisbol aficionados* had seen quite a game.

IF IT DOES NOT HELP YOU…

Miguel returned, at last. A week had passed since he had set out to find and retrieve a half dozen cows who had run in the wrong direction due to a horrific storm with thunder and lightning. The noisy storm was such the feebleminded cows must have thought, *"We are as good as dead!"*

The family was delighted to see him! Yaqui Indians inhabit the Valparaiso Mountains, part of the Sierra Madre Occidental range, so the family feared for Miguel's life.

The ladies served Miguel dinner while his younger brothers milked the recovered cows.

When Miguel finished his hearty meal, and his brothers returned, Miguel drew out his adventure up the mountain in search of the *"loco"* cows.

"It was my turn to go in search of the crazy cattle. Mother packed food for a week to ten days. My bedding, extra clothes, another pair of boots, rifle, ammunition, shovel, pike, and cooking utensils required me to be a sure-footed burro as my beast of burden. I rode horseback.

"I headed out before sunrise the day after the late evening storm. Six cows were missing when we went out to tend the stock after the thunder/lightning subsided. I quickly picked up the tracks. Tracking was made accessible due to the herd and the mud.

"Unfortunately, the cows aimed for higher ground, Yerba Buena, the highest peak. (*The family ranch was named after this peak.*) Even the most inexperienced cowboy knows cows are not known for their intelligence.

"I feared the Yaqui Indians had already come upon the cows and butchered some. Also, I carelessly slashed my left hand while opening a can of beans. My stupid slip made matters worse. It was not a severe injury, but it limited the use of my left hand. I managed to wrap it well enough to be of some help to my right hand. I went to my makeshift bed, reliving my blunder.

"The following morning, I woke up shivering. I feared an infection from my cut, but I took caution to use my turtle-neck, white thermal shirt to curtail my shivering. I layered by wearing my heavy, black shirt—it would absorb the sun's rays and keep me warm. This clothing gave me a distinct appearance, quickly noted by the Yaqui Indians later.

"The following afternoon, I came upon our cows. They were penned up in a box canyon. The Indians were milking them. I was glad because the cows would suffer from not being milked. I quickly scanned for weapons and was greatly relieved to see none.

"Now, my apprehension shifted to proof of ownership of the stock. Ownership papers were not my concern since the Indians probably could not read them. I stalled for time by tinkering with my supplies.

"The Indians, dressed in colorless clothes, wearing straw hats and *huaraches* on their feet, checked my horse and donkey. Of course, what a fool I was! They were comparing brands! I felt shame! Their intelligence should not have surprised me; they live by their wits in these cruel mountains.

"Now that they saw all of me, they quickly knelt with heads bowed. Embarrassed, I motioned them to stand. They led me to their village; the cows brought up the rear.

"As we arrived at their village, everyone stopped doing whatever they were doing and stood at attention for a second before falling to their knees. The tallest man in the group of approximately 50 people appeared. He was well over six feet tall. This Indian stood out from all other Yaquis who were about a head shorter than him.

"Again, I motioned for the villagers to rise, which they did. I was baffled as to why they kept kneeling whenever they saw me for the first time.

"The women rapidly prepared some food, and we all ate a simple meal of beans and corn tortillas. I ate with a smile on my face wanting not to insult them. They readily accepted my eating with them as a great compliment.

"When I finished eating, the village people approached me again and fell to their knees. I did not comprehend what they expected, yet I was sure I had to do something. The tall one, who I could tell was their leader, came up and arranged my collar after softly touching my injured left hand.

"Just then, I knew what they were waiting for me to do! They thought I was a *Padre*, a Father of the Catholic Church! They were waiting for me to give them communion.

"What to do? What to do? They must get regular visits from a *Padre* and thus recognize the sacramental bread, also called communion bread, wafer, or host they consume at communion.

"Then it came to me—mother's toasted flour tortillas. Boy, was I glad the bread can be leavened or unleavened? I broke them into pieces, and I was ready. But what was I supposed to utter before each person received the communion bread? Father spoke those words in Latin, and I could not recall them.

I was safe; undoubtedly, the Yaquis did not know the words either.

"So before placing a tortilla chip on the tongue of each Yaqui Indian, I pronounced the following words, 'IF IT DOES NOT HELP YOU, MAY IT NOT HARM YOU!'"

A DOG NAMED 'WHY'

The family lived in rural, pastoral Brownsville, Texas. A large, two-story house surrounded by a large citrus orchard was home. More than half of the sixty acres were navel oranges. Grapefruit, tangerines, and lemons completed the orchard.

Greg and Mary owned a milk cow, pigs, chickens, and an occasional goat. Hence, the family had food and could sell milk, cheese, and eggs.

Yet, the parents would not allow the four children to get what they wished. The youngsters pleaded for a dog. The parents held their ground and would not consent to have a dog on their little *"Ranchito."*

Their main objection to a dog was its danger to the other animals, especially the mother hens with baby chicks.

Greg and Mary agreed to protect from thievery the citrus crop in exchange for living in the only home on the property. And, though the home's only indoor utility was a cold-water pump, it was nicer than where they lived.

The day came when the home/citrus owner strongly suggested a dog for added security for his valuable navel oranges. So, to put a period on his strong recommendation, he returned to his vehicle, withdrew a beautiful puppy, and left.

With their backs to the wall, Greg and Mary had no choice! The children had their dog!

Still, the father wanted control of the new situation. He alone would name the dog! Furthermore, Greg had already picked the name.

At this point, all the children inquired about the puppy's name.

Greg answered, "Why."

The children misread their dad's intonation. They thought he was upset at them for asking. The children looked at each other and then at their father.

Rosemary, the youngest, asked, "Daddy, what is the puppy's name?"

Once again, Greg repeated, "Why." And, one more time, the children looked at each other. They were sure their father was angry at THEM for having a dog forced on him.

This time Carmen, the eldest, used her position in the family to ask, "Dad, we want to know the puppy's name."

For the third time, Greg answered, "Why." At this time, Mary was in tears with laughter.

The children were more confused than ever, and their father's face gave them no clue. The children were not about to give up. Their eyes all went to Joe. They considered him the family's favorite.' This assumption was not valid. The parents viewed Joe as the most trustworthy, reliable, and dependable.

Thus, the oldest boy, Joe, braved to ask, "Dad, we want to know what you named the dog?"

The children intently watched their father's face for a hint when he answered, "Why."

Simultaneously, the children yelled, "WHY! WHY! WHY! The dog's name is "WHY!" They fell to the ground laughing and repeating, "WHY! WHY! WHY! WHY! WHY! WHY! WHY!"

OH! What fun they would have with their dog named "WHY!"

Tumbleweed Christmas

The robust and stiff wind would not ease up, much less stop.

It had been ruthless for over ten hours and showed no sign of letting up. The wind was nothing new, but it was much more potent today. And, worse yet, it was accompanied by blinding dust!

Terrace Mountains was not a place anyone would prefer to live, not if he had a choice.

Rod and Grace had come here because they had an obligation to fulfill. The mining company Terrace Mountains Silver (TMS) had covered the costs of their last two years of college education once their savings had run out. That agreement stipulated: The young couple was committed to teaching for three years.

Terrace Mountains Silver was a tiny hamlet. The only people living here were miners, their families, and TMS's superintendent and manager. Less than fifty people lived in well-built, three-room shacks measuring about forty by thirty. Only the mine superintendent and manager had living quarters worthy of mention, yet, they were not much. Thus, their wives and children refused to live here. Logan, Utah, was their permanent home, more than three hours away.

Sixteen men worked the silver mine, which had seen better days. But if there was silver and a profit to be made, Colin Worthington was not about to leave it behind, no matter how small.

All but four of the miners were married. Their wives worked at the company store or the laundry, while two worked as teaching assistants and kept the books for the mine.

Twenty-two students attended the school, which included grades 1st through high school. It was near impossible to get teachers to come here to teach. That is why Mr. Worthington would make good for the schooling of teachers in return for them being willing to live and teach there for anywhere from two to 5 years, depending on the college costs compensated by Mr. Worthington. By law, he had to make available schooling at the location so long as six school-age children lived at the tiny hamlet.

Years before, three shacks had been placed to form a giant Y. The top area of the Y had an umbrella-like covering as protection from severe weather. A back door led to the open clearing, giving the students an outdoor feeling. One of the shacks housed the 1st through fifth graders. In the middle cabin, sixth through 9th graders—Junior High—could be found in the middle cabin. The high school students occupied the third hut.

Terrace Mountains Silver was slightly over 180 miles from Logan, Utah. Interstate 84 and State Highway 30 were the main roads. Still, after leaving Highway 30, it took another hour on a rough, unpaved road to make it to the mine. Enough sand and gravel made the road navigable even in the rain.

This remote, rural location proved a terrible hardship for the tiny hamlet. The weekly assignment of TMS's superintendent and the manager was food, clothing, pharmaceutical supplies, and miscellaneous necessities. Sixteen-foot trucks were used to bring the supplies. The two men drove the trucks after the weekend visits with their families. Understandably, the products sold at the mine's general store were priced quite a bit higher than what they sold for in Logan.

This situation was disadvantageous since all miners quickly became indebted to the company store. Most families had little money left at the end of each month and thought, "Next month will be different." Yet, something else always came up to devour hard-earned dollars. Though not thrilled at their outlook, they liked living far from violence, drugs, and the many other negatives which came with city living. The miner families were unique in the love and protection of their children.

When the new miners started working at the mine, they paid no mind to their being in the red the first few months, thinking this was temporary. They justified, "We expect this upside-down situation since we are getting a new start, and there are one-time-only costs to be incurred."

Now, realizing their state, the miners were preoccupied with their finances. It seems the only people not downcast were Rod and Grace. They were making the best of their situation.

For as long as they can remember, they wanted to be teachers. Rod and Grace had gone to school together since kindergarten.

In Logan, Utah State University was their choice for a college education. College scholarships each had won paid for the first year. They married after that first year and worked all summer long for their college costs for the second year, but the money ran out, and they had to take Mr. Worthington's offer for free education to agree to teach at the mining school.

Yes, of course, Rod and Grace were paid for teaching, but the salary for a first-year teacher is pitiful. Still, the couple was determined to make the best of a deplorable situation. They loved children and teaching, and, above all, they knew they had to be cheerful. Rod and Grace were determined to help the tiny hamlet change things with some happiness. As the saying goes, the couple saw their environment *"...through rose-colored glasses"*.

The school was in session when the wind became a fierce dust storm. Everyone thought it was just the common wind they knew.

But this day's wind intensified and started to pick up dust. In no time, it was impossible to see within a few feet. The school was held captive. The teachers and assistants thought it better to ride it out, fearing the danger of allowing the students to make it home. The homes were about two hundred yards from the school, but one could see only a few feet—two hundred yards may have been a million miles. The only thing one could see was a dark-tan wall of dust.

Since the back of the cabins touched the sides and created an enclosed patio with an umbrella-like covering, the students and adults exited through the back doors and walked across the patio to the primary-grades building.

The adults thought it would be less scary for the younger ones if the older students came to the building familiar to the youngsters. There was plenty of room, and the younger students would have their older siblings there to help comfort them.

Rod phoned the store, the office, and the laundromat to tell them not to worry about the children. The entire school settled in for, what was thought, would be a few hours of discomfort.

Grace considered the bathroom usage not a problem since they were in the covered patio area, but it could pose a severe issue if the dust worsened.

The group was now set. All they could do was wait. Storytelling seemed the best way to wait out the dust storm. But after a couple of hours, the younger ones began to cry. Rod and Grace countered that by proposing the group sing Christmas songs.

They were shocked the children did not know any of the songs! It turned out; that the mining camp had not celebrated Christmas in years. December 25 was just another day in the bleak tiny hamlet.

{The school did not celebrate any of the holidays, choosing instead to let out early in May. By skipping the holidays, the teachers had time to further their education to improve their teaching. But if they had fulfilled their teaching obligation to Mr. Worthington, teachers usually left to look for other teaching positions elsewhere. Also, many children went off to live with relatives during the summer.}

Rod and Grace aimed to teach them the songs one by one. They sang each one until they were pleased with the memorization and tone of the song and moved on to the next one. Once the group mastered several songs, they began decorating for the holiday, only a few weeks away.

Shortly after 8:00 PM, the wind and dust stopped at long last. Three of the older high-school boys volunteered to walk out and look around. When they returned with a "clear-and-calm" report, the adults took no chances and organized the students in groups, with the adults and the three older boys as leaders. They hurried to their homes.

The community was furious that Rod and Grace had taught Christmas songs to the children. They called a meeting to let them know just how they felt. They were so upset at the teachers; that they would have fired Rod and Grace if they had had the authority. "It is painful enough to live in this area. The children do not need to learn of 'foolish' celebrations without sound basis."

Parents objected to the idea of a "*Santa Claus*" and gifts when they barely could make a living. After an hour of angry banter and accusations, Rod and Grace agreed with the parents, letting them know Christ was not born in December. Also, the Bible does not mention celebrating birthdays. Still, since the children had this in mind and it had helped save them from a horrible day, why not celebrate a day and call it *"OUR HOLIDAY"* instead of Christmas? Rod and Grace said, "A negative vote on a celebration will cause more misery and develop a chasm between parents and children." For the majority of one, the teachers had their way.

Perhaps due to the dust storm and the Christmas singing, the students were in much better spirits in the days before Christmas. (Thanks to Rod and Grace, the school had always been positive, but now they were a team.) Since the primary classroom had already been decorated, the students pulled together and finished decorating the Junior-High and high school classrooms.

The high school students, especially the boys, hesitated to participate in the decoration. Rod came up with an idea.

The boys would be responsible for coming up with the Christmas tree. At first, the boys loudly protested. (No matter how hard everyone tried to remember to call it "OUR HOLIDAY," it kept coming up "Christmas" instead. Even the parents would let it slip.)

They were told their assignment covered biology, math, chemistry, geography, art, and history. Rod told them there was a solution to the lack of trees in the area, and the answer involved at least the six fields he had mentioned. (Rod could have added music but did not want to make it more complicated than it already was.) It was up to them to determine the answer and develop a suitable Christmas tree.

The boys accepted the challenge and set to work on it immediately. After a few hours of thinking, discussing, designing, and joking, they asked if they could roam the desolate area outside the classroom. They were surprised at Rod's delight at their suggestion. He encouraged them by telling them they were headed in the right direction.

Immediately, the other students wanted to go outside, too. Grace asked the remaining students to do what the older boys had done. She wanted them to group and come up with ideas. Grace told them the main answer was out there, but part of the answer was in each classroom and the company store. She counted on them to help their older siblings find a Christmas tree like no other. Grace inspired the children to "…think outside the box. Come up with something never heard or seen."

It took no time for the younger students to give up on thinking about a Christmas tree. Next, Grace asked them to draw a Christmas tree; but their drawing could not be of a real, living evergreen tree. They were to draw a tree made of whatever came to mind. Grace told them they could use anything they wanted and hinted at "items you use daily and objects thrown in the garbage daily."

After a while, Grace asked to see each drawing, even if it was unfinished. For example, the student mentioned the object he was using—tin cans.

Third-grader Brittney came up with the idea of tumbleweeds as a basis for her tree. When asked why, Brittney said, "Because the wind blew hundreds, maybe thousands of them all around us. But mostly because it was the easiest to draw, and I could finish faster." All the students cheered and headed out to tell the older boys.

The younger group was surprised, yet pleased, to see that the high school boys had already built a small Christmas tree out of tumbleweeds. It was what they called their *"prototype."*

Right then and there, the entire school started bouncing ideas of how to construct a unique Christmas tree ever.

The students realized they needed gloves or socks instead of gloves, long sleeves, and long pants to avoid getting the tiny, irritating stickers that the tumbleweeds carried.

As the next day was a Saturday, the parents joined in the fun of gathering tumbleweeds. The parent's willingness shocked

Rod and Grace, especially after reacting to the teachers introducing Christmas songs to the students.

Saturday was usually the busiest day for the company store, but it closed until the evening.

The same thing applied to the laundromat. (The laundromat is typically closed on Sunday and Monday. Mr. Worthington required all miners to wear company pants and shirts with the company's logo and each miner's name embroidered on the shirt and the trousers. The families' laundry was also taken care of by the laundromat.)

No one recalled ever having a day like this "*tumbleweed-gathering day*." Yes, the mine had had some deadly accidents where the whole community gathered, yet, this was always a stressful, anxious time. It usually ended with immense relief for some families but profound grief for others. Minor recognition was why Colin Worthington wanted the miner's name embroidered on both shirts and pants.

By early afternoon, the group had collected an enormous number of tumbleweeds. Delighted with their effort, the community took a timeout to go home and fix sandwiches and sundries for a picnic lunch before the tumbleweeds. While eating, they discussed the best way to decorate and form the tree.

Never had the village felt so close. Long after the hamlet had agreed to assemble their Christmas tree, the families lingered, enjoying each other's company. Soon, a softball game started where the school children played against the parents. It was a day to remember!

Come Sunday, the *"Tumbleweed Christmas"* project started. The females decorated the tumbleweeds by spray painting the lower part of the tumbleweeds green, and the upper half was sprayed with cans of snow spray.

Rod and Grace had found dozens of the green spray paint cans and even more snow cans. The previous teachers had ordered them at the beginning of the school year, anticipating using them at a Christmas the hamlet disapproved of celebrating.

However, there would not be enough cans of either the green paint or the snow, so the tree design, which Robert and Erin did, would have to show the unseen interior as unpainted. (Though the project was fun, the teachers incorporated as much schooling as possible. The students saw firsthand what Rod had mentioned about using school subjects in their tree project.)

The males, appointed with the Tumbleweed Tree construction, used even the youngest boys. Timmy and Eddie had the role of keeping track of the number of tumbleweeds.

When the *Tumbleweed Tree* "grew" too tall for the men to add tumbleweeds, they got permission to use the mine's crane. At that point, the boys were relegated to just toting the plants. From there, the men assembled the uppermost part of the tree.

When the last tumbleweed was placed, it was late but not dark. Everyone waited for the crane operator and the bucket man to join them. They then started to applaud and cheer. The parents hugged and squeezed their youngest children. The women could not contain themselves; tears ran freely.

No one could be blamed for letting their emotions go for the *beautiful Tumbleweed Tree*. Every person had helped, making the entire community proud of itself. Those who owned cameras took pictures—lots of photos.

Though the tiny hamlet had finished a monumental project that united them, they woke up sad the following day! They didn't understand this feeling. Confused and upset at their downtrodden mood, some came out of their cabins and walked toward their giant *Tumbleweed Tree*. (The parents may have felt guilty about continually calling it Christmas instead of "OUR HOLIDAY.")

Did the *Tumbleweed Tree* have the answer to their sentiment? Were they disappointed at not being able to provide gifts for their children? They wanted an explanation!

The parents making their way to the tree were primarily men. Nonetheless, they greeted each other with a guilty nod and continued walking to the tree. **AND THEN, THEY NOTICED IT!!!!**

Wrapped gifts covered the ground all around the *Tumbleweed Tree*. The men looked at each other and shrugged their shoulders.

One of the men read one or two packages, dropped them, and ran full speed to the community's cabins. He was too slow; someone had already switched on the *"disaster siren."*

The remainder of the community, still in the cabins, rushed out and headed for the mine, only to see men waving at them to come to the *Tumbleweed Tree*!

Relieved, puzzled, and excited, the crowd hurried to their tree. Now, the remainder of the residents saw hundreds of wrapped gifts! Indeed, there must be at least one gift for each resident!

Someone would pick up a package with glee and yell out the name inscribed on it. Names were being shouted out while the sirens were blaring. It was chaos!

Floyd, the most prominent man in the group, who also was blessed with a booming voice, asked everyone to stand still. Floyd signaled the disaster siren to be turned off and spoke, "I have the loudest voice here. If no one objects, I will take the place of GIVER."

Floyd requested the aid of some "helpers" to assist him. He huddled five women "helpers" and then whispered for them to bring him the gifts addressed to the youngest first.

Somehow every person got what he wanted. Furthermore, each got three gifts.

Only Rod and Grace knew the origin of the gifts.

After the teachers learned the school would be allowed to celebrate Christmas, they reached out to Costco, J C Penny, Sears, Target, and Walmart, and the stores came through with "flying colors."

That was the first of many years the generous businesses provided gifts for the mining hamlet. And, year after year, Rod and Grace saw that everyone received what he needed.

(The following year, the celebration WAS called "OUR HOLIDAY." And it remained all the time Rod and Grace taught school there. The tradition of gathering tumbleweeds stayed, though it was renamed "THE MOUND." "The Mound" was not decorated. It was set on fire and blazed during the presentation of the gifts.)

In the following weeks, the students learned how the subjects Rod had mentioned applied to their education. They traced the origin of the tumbleweed from Russia to South Dakota, brought in apparently in flaxseed imported by Ukrainian farmers in the 1870s.

It is also known as the *"Russian thistle"* because it is native to Russia's arid steppes of the Ural Mountains. Tumbleweeds can be as small as a soccer ball and as large as a Volkswagen beetle. Thus, the students used biology, geography, history, and art.

The spread of the tumbleweed in the U.S.A. was charted. Math was used in counting the spray cans necessary for the project—total ounces--, tree height, width, and volume. Geometry was used due to the angles to construct their "pride and joy."

Chemicals in the paint and the artificial snow were researched. The learning went on and on. New vocabulary was acquired. Note-taking skills were used. Bookkeeping, accounting, and money lessons were learned.

As for music, *The Sons of the Pioneers* made the song *Tumbling Tumbleweeds* famous in the 1940s. So, of course, the teachers played that song repeatedly.

Talented and creative, Rod and Grace brought joy to schooling that otherwise would have been dry and boring. Even the primary-grade children were engaged in so much learning. They especially loved the art involved in charts, graphs, and maps of the nations where the tumbleweed grows.

Rod and Grace not only fulfilled their three-year agreement with Mr. Worthington, but they also stayed on for years. And year after year, the tiny hamlet constructed its mound of tumbleweeds.

If you are ever in that area around the winter solstice, it will be worth your drive to see and have your picture taken at the foot of the *"Tumbleweed Mound."*

ANY FOOL CAN RIDE A BIKE!

It was unusual for the Spooners to eat meat. The family lived in rural Brownsville, Texas, and had no utilities. Thus, meat purchased or gifted had to be consumed promptly, or it would spoil.

On a Saturday in the summer of 1954, their closest neighbor, who lived over a mile away, brought them a rack of pork ribs. Wilma, Mrs. Spooner, asked Wil, her only son, to walk to the country store two miles away and buy a ketchup bottle. She stated, "Ribs taste much better with ketchup."

The path to the small country store ran parallel to a wide irrigation canal and was rugged as all get out--barely fit for walking. Also, parallel but on the opposite side of the canal was a thickly wooded strip. And on the edge of the heavy woods was an enormous lake/reservoir.

The father said he would go instead of Wil, and Mr. Spooner intended to ride Wil's 26-inch Western Flyer bicycle. Both mother and son remarked that Wilford had never ridden a bike. Mr. Spooner answered, "Any fool can ride a bike!"

Once again, Wilma and Wil pointed out the impossibility of riding the bike on the 'canal' path.

Wilford returned, "I do not intend to use the path; instead, I will use the roads."

That route was much, much longer. It was approximately 5 miles, of which the first three were dirt roads. The other two miles were paved but dangerous for a non-bike rider like Wilford due to the many vehicles which traveled on it.

Nonetheless, Mr. Spooner was persistent. He took off, fell a few times, and wobbled for a hundred yards before steadying the bike.

Still laughing, Mrs. Spooner set to cook the spare ribs, so they would be ready when her husband, she hoped, returned with the ketchup.

Wilford was in excellent shape, for the five miles were taxing for an experienced rider, which Wilford was not. It took a lot more energy for a "new' bike rider like Wilford. Eventually, he made it to the store, purchased the glass-bottled ketchup, and returned. *{This is 1954, and glass was just about the only way to package items.}*

Mr. Spooner held the bottle in his left hand, limiting him to using only the right hand while peddling his bike. This handicap proved too much. The stubborn, two-wheeled monster refused to cooperate, so Mr. reluctantly placed the glass jar under his shirt and started anew.

Down went Mr. Spooner, bicycle and all! Wilford looked around to see if anyone had seen his shameful tumble. Then he assessed his damage. Mr. Spooner thought his shirt was soaked with ketchup but was wrong! The bottle broke while pressed against Wilford's chest, impacting the paved road. Wilford had sustained numerous cuts on his chest. There was more blood than ketchup on his soaked shirt!

An older man stopped to assist Mr. Spooner. He ordered him to sit while he carefully pulled out the more significant shards of glass. After he finished, he tore a towel he carried in his pickup into strips and wrapped them around Wilford's chest.

The kind-hearted man loaded Mr. Spooner's bicycle on the bed of his pickup and drove Wilford home.

His family was worried and thus delighted to see him climb out of a pickup they did not recognize.

Wil helped the good Samaritan take the bike out of the pickup bed.

Wilma carefully removed the tiny shards the older man had missed. After, she cleaned the wounds with rubbing alcohol and bandaged the injured area.

Now that Mr. Spooner was taken care of, he cheerfully asked,

"Am I worthy of at least one spare rib, even though I cannot

ride a bike?"

NO FISHING HOOK

Growing up in a secluded area of Brownsville, Texas, was an experience to behold for an adventurous, curious nine-year-old boy. The year was 1953, the good old days.

Ross delighted in roaming the areas surrounding his home. A vast reservoir/lake was located a mere 150 yards from the front door of his house. The Rio Grande stocked the water and most fish to the lake. In turn, the water was the primary source for irrigation in the southernmost area of Cameron County.

A large variety of fish inhabited the reservoir. Yet, the most numerous species were catfish, lake trout, and gar. Ross's favorite was the colorful perch. Many other freshwater creatures could be found here, but the only other ones Ross could name were turtles—the crystal-clear water made for an aquarium-like atmosphere.

Beautiful homes with spacious landscaping filled the shore across Ross's swimming spot. He often saw men and boys fishing from canoes or their boat docks. Of course, due to his age and his upbringing, Ross did not know what they were doing at first.

When Ross asked his dad, he explained fishing down to the bait and hook. Ross begged for such an apparatus, but his dad answered, "No, with all the trees and bushes between the canal and lake, you should be able to find a nice pole. You can have some of my less coarse, sturdy cord, and I will buy you a hook. What you work to make will be better and more rewarding since you made it yourself."

 (A thirty-foot wide irrigation canal ran precisely in the center between the lake and Ross's home. Dense woods separated the canal from the lake.)

Ross waited for days, and when his dad did not produce a hook as he had promised, he complained to his mother, who told him, "Your dad can get a hook only at a certain store, and we don't go into town but once a week. Brownsville is miles away, and without a car, your dad cannot just go anytime you want. Here, take these straight pins and make your fishing hooks. It should not be that difficult."

Ross put his heart into fashioning a fitting fishing pole despite the pins. He failed miserably, as repeatedly, the fish would not get hooked securely or make haste with bait and makeshift hook. His mother had given him small flour dough balls to use as bait.

It was frustrating seeing the fish plainly in the calm, clear water. Ross had the brilliant idea of using his finger as the hook. He cautiously placed the dough around his index finger and lowered it into the clean, lucid water.

Wow! Immediately, a hit! A small catfish tried to snatch the bait and got hooked by Ross's finger. Unbelievable luck had been with Ross as he flipped the runty fish onto the dry ground.

Ross's mind went crazy with thoughts such as, "I can feed the entire family with all the fish I will catch. We can have fish every day. No more beans and tortillas!"

He dipped his arm into the calm water again. This time Ross was not so lucky. A sizable catfish got a hold of his finger, and Ross felt pain just like he felt when vaccinated. He hated shots. Impulsively, Ross withdrew his arm from the water and looked at his wounded, bleeding finger.

Ross placed his little catch in his back pocket, for his hands were occupied. One hand was injured, and the other was holding the bleeding finger. He headed home.

Already, Ross knew what he would be doing tomorrow. He was confident his mother would nurse his finger so he could fish with his homemade bow and arrow.

{PS: When Ross related this story to his eighth-grade buddies in Cantua Creek, California, six years later, they, who had the luxury of much more experienced fathers, informed Ross of his crimes. Fishing by finger is called **'noodling'** *and is illegal, as is using floor dough, thus making Ross one of the youngest criminals ever. Ross did not rightly know if there were 'WANTED' posters of himself back in Texas! Then and then,*

Ross decided to stay out of Texas until the statute of limitation

expired the next year.}

THE DOG HAS TO GO

Joe and Ross were visibly troubled. Their mother, María, had earlier caught Gorilla in the hen house. That made the third time the jet-black, longhaired female Australian shepherd had gotten at the hens' eggs. Just days before, Gregorio, the boys' father, had stated, "The dog has to go the next time she gets in the eggs!"

Any minute now, they expected their dad home from work. The boys feared for Gorilla. Knowing how strong-willed their father was, Joe and Ross dreaded what their dad would do to their beloved dog, for Gorilla had provoked Gregorio's wrath for the last time.

Deep attachment intertwined Joe, Ross, and Gorilla. One could not ask for a more exemplary dog. As a watchdog, there were none better. The female sheepdog was exceptional around the younger children. She would not allow the youngsters anywhere close to water, of which there was *"way too much too close to the house,"* as María repeatedly complained. Gorilla's shepherding instinct came alive whenever she sensed a child heading for danger.

All that changed when Gorilla discovered a taste for the hens' eggs. No matter how faithful the dog was, the Sánchez family could ill afford its new habit. The eggs were crucial to the family—a total of eight members. The Sánchez consumed about a dozen daily; the remainder were sold to add to Gregorio's weekly salary.

Joe and Ross's thoughts drifted back to when Gorilla saved them from drowning by alerting their dad about their predicament. Now, they were dreading her fate. How long had they owned Gorilla? The boys could not be sure. Was it three? Or four years? (This year, 1954, made it four years.) Gorilla never caused the family trouble until the *'dropped egg.'*

Ross collected the eggs on that fateful day. Usually, his mom was the one who gathered the eggs. Since María was quick and sure-handed while picking the eggs, her extreme focus and care did not show. At least, it was not evident to Ross. María's husband, Gregorio, bragged about his wife's "soft hands"—never a dropped or crushed egg!

After a couple of lessons, María thought Ross could gather the eggs, as she had plenty else to do. Sadly, Ross's lackadaisical attitude produced failure in this exacting task.

At first, Ross did very well until he began to think there was nothing to collecting the eggs. His lack of focus and overconfidence caused him to fumble an egg. Ross failed in his attempt to recover the egg in mid-air. It fell to the ground and cracked!

Quickly, Ross looked around to see if anyone had witnessed his error. Only Gorilla had witnessed Ross's clumsiness, and she could keep a secret. Ross was determined to get rid of the evidence of his misdeed.

Childlike, Ross reasoned, Gorilla could eat the evidence without leaving a trace. BAD MISTAKE!

He called Gorilla to enter the hen house and eat the broken egg. (It never dawned on Ross that Gorilla had never been allowed inside the hen house for a good reason.) Too late, the deed was done.

Ross laid the basket of eggs down and picked up the small shell fragments which Gorilla had not consumed. He walked them over to the citrus orchard to bury them.

While he was gone, Gorilla went to work on the eggs in the basket. It was an awful mess! There was nothing else to do except report what Gorilla had done. Ross was afraid to admit his part in the fiasco. He placed the guilt on Gorilla, a poor beast who could not defend itself.

Days later, Gorilla dug her way into the hen house to get the eggs. That was the day Gregorio declared Gorilla would be done away with if she got into the eggs one more time.

Facing the loss of the blameless dog, Ross confessed. Gregorio stated it did not make any difference; *"once a dog gets the taste of eggs, it will not stop."* Now, Gorilla was not a pet; she was a liability. The dog would have to go.

When Gregorio got home, María walked quickly to meet him in the front yard. Joe and Ross hurried to hear the conversation. As María handed Gregorio a water glass, she turned to order the boys away. She wanted a private talk with her husband.

When the couple finished conversing, they went in different directions. María went into the house, while Gregorio went into the tool shed.

With a rope in hand, Gregorio called Gorilla to him. Being the obedient and well-trained dog she was, Gorilla quickly obeyed. Man and dog walked across the irrigation-canal bridge, turned right, and along the path parallel to the canal. The narrow, densely wooded strip blocked a clear view of the lake below on their left.

Where were they going? Why the rope?

Joe and Ross did not heed their mom's cries to return to the house. They were busy running after their dad and their beloved dog. When the boys caught up, they asked what their dad aimed to do with their beloved Gorilla.

Gregorio crossly answered, "Go home! Gorilla is no longer your dog. She will never again be your dog. I am taking her to one of my workers. He has no animals of any kind and no close neighbors." (Gregorio was foreman of a crew of men who cleared the irrigation canals of brush for Cameron County Irrigation District in Brownsville, Texas.)

Joe and Ross did not understand their father's tone—he sounded as if he was angry at himself.

Gregorio changed his tone and continued, "I am asking you nicely to return home and stay there. Think of all the good memories you have of Gorilla. Always remember her that way. Now, go home."

Gregorio stood motionless as he watched his boys head home.

When the grieved father heard his boys' bawling, he resumed his walk to Gorilla's new home.

With no one to console them, Joe and Ross comforted each other by placing an arm over their shoulder and continued their painful walk home.

ALLIGATOR GAR

Brothers Jimmy John Algee and Roe John Algee lost their swimming hole! The lake/reservoir was near gone! What happened to all the water? The boys wondered.

Here and there, water areas still existed. Due to their indentation, those locations were more profound than most of the lake floor. The lake had transformed from a gorgeous body of water to a massive muddy muck and no longer supplied irrigation water for farmers in Cameron County, Texas.

{Since the boys' father worked for Cameron County Irrigation District, they knew the Río Grande supplied water to this reservoir. They did not know that the river's flow had dropped below the level where massive pumps siphoned water were situated. Their father gave them that information that evening.}

Seeing those spots which still contained water, the boys hoped, "There might be such a place close to the shore." So, they looked for such a site, which was difficult, for the lake's west border was framed by thickly wooded patches.

On the other hand, the east border was the complete opposite. High above the lake, large, beautiful homes with picture-perfect landscaping enclosed the lake's east shore. The neatly manicured and enormous lawns sloped gradually to meet the lakeshore. Each home had its boat dock. Jimmy John and Roe John envied those who lived in those homes, for they thought their set was like a postcard—or a setting only seen in the movies.

As far as they knew, their home was the only one on the west border, and from where it sat, they could not see the lake. There were two reasons for that: (1) their view was blocked by the heavy-wooded strip, and (2) the lake was much lower than their home.

Then the boys eyed the most prominent water area they had yet encountered through an opening in the woods. They worked their way down to that choice *'swimming* hole' through the scrub brush, mesquites, and manzanitas.

They had almost reached what the brothers thought would be their next swimming hole when Jimmy John and Roe John came upon a small clearing where lay the most prominent fish they had ever seen. In truth, the *'monster'* was gutted and looked quite like an alligator but devoid of the legs the alligator has. Roe John pointed out this body was more cylindrical than the squatty shape of the alligator, or maybe, it just appeared that way because it was gutted. It was approximately 9 feet long, and in its snout/mouth were dozens of fishing hooks, small and large—indications of failed attempts to land this beast.

Immediately, Jimmy John,10, expressed apprehension about swimming in the body of water only yards from this carcass. His older brother Roe John,13, pointed out they could not tell if that giant fish had come from that large swimming hole. The monster could have been brought here to gut so as not to bother getting rid of the carcass. Roe John pointed out the bridge over the lake less than a hundred yards away. This bridge provided easy access to where they found the fish if it was a fish! It looked prehistoric to the young, naive boys.

The boys' '*new*' swimming area was much larger than their old one. Their old swimming hole was half the size of a football field. Its left side stopped at a vast but beautiful water lily area. The area to the right ended where fallen and dead trees rested underwater. The boys' father and his co-workers, who all worked for the Cameron County Irrigation District, had cleared the swimming area. Only one large tree branch lay just above the water. The boys used it as a diving platform or to rest in the water. The swimming hole's depth went down to twenty feet. Tommy John Algee, the boys' father, habitually reminded them to stay out of the water lilies and the area cluttered with dead trees lest they get entangled underwater and drown.

The promising new swimming area was rectangular and about the size of a football field. It posed no visible dangers, but its depth was only 5 to 7 feet, and its water was nowhere as clear as the water in the old swimming hole.

Roe John quickly jumped in at the swimming hole they had spotted from above. Jimmy John dreaded entering the water. His thoughts were on the giant fish. After much persuasion, Roe John finally convinced Jimmy John to jump in and begin a game of *'tag'* underwater. He volunteered to be *'it.'*

Jimmy John went underwater and searched for the perfect place to hide. He found an underwater bush and crunched behind it, holding his breath. When Jimmy John needed to surface and get a fresh breath, little brother spied big brother swimming underwater toward him. He gathered himself into a tight ball to conceal himself better behind his bush. Only it was NOT Roe John!

A fish more enormous than the one the boys saw on that clearing was coming for Jimmy John! He could hold his breath no longer when the fish suddenly turned and disappeared. Jimmy John surfaced as fast as he could and swam to shore.

Standing on the shore, Jimmy John hurriedly looked for his brother. Roe John was nowhere in sight! Panicky, Jimmy John ran back and forth on the shore.

Little Jimmy was relieved when his big brother surfaced. He screamed for Roe John to get out of the water, which he promptly did.

Roe John, unhappy at his brother's cowardice, proclaimed the fish would not attack him. Again, he reminded his brother the fish was more scared of them. No matter! Jimmy John refused to enter the water again!

Later that evening, when Tommy John came home from work, he told his boys the fish they saw was an ALLIGATOR GAR, and, yes, Roe John was right. The gar would flee from them instead of attacking them.

Tommy John continued his boys' education, "Alligator gars range from 2.5 feet to 10 feet, though some have been reported as large as 13 feet, not here in Texas. The gar might grow that large in Florida, Central and South America, and the West Indies. Adults weigh easily over 200 pounds to as much as 360. The one you saw alive is surviving because gars have a swim bladder connected to their esophagus, which acts as a lung, allowing the gar you saw to breathe in stagnant water with little oxygen. I doubt it will survive much longer. It is a captive where it is now with little food. It eats live and dead fish, small turtles, and frogs which likely are in short supply. The best we can do for it is kill it quickly so he will not suffer a slow, painful death. Hopefully, I will speak to my co-workers this Saturday and plan to do just that."

The boys were impressed and proud of their father's education—he had finished eighth grade! No wonder, thought the boys: their dad wanted them to be the first in the family to graduate high school. Why! With a high school education, the boys' prospects would be limitless!

Jimmy John and Roe John went to bed, thankful for a loving father who cared for them and the animals.

THE SHIRT OFF HIS BACK

While Gregorio serviced the pumps which siphoned water out of the Río Grande, he saw movement in the broad, quick-moving river one hundred yards from his location. He stopped what he was doing to get a better look, for it appeared a swimmer was in trouble.

Thankfully, no! Instead, Gregorio witnessed a failed attempt to retrieve a bundle. The current quickly took the parcel out of reach of the swimmer. Gregorio resumed his work.

The sizable pumps draw water out of the Río Grande and release it into a canal about twenty feet wide and 12 feet deep. The canal carries the river water to an enormous lake reservoir. From here, the Río Grande water is channeled into thirty-foot-wide canals from which farmers withdraw the precious liquid to irrigate their crops. Cameron County Irrigation District is charged with the task.

These pumps and Gregorio's home are on the remotest southern border of Cameron County in Brownsville, Texas. Their location is miles southwest of the border crossing between Brownsville, Texas, and *Matamoros, Tamaulipas,* Mexico. A colossal bridge connects the cities.

Minutes later, Gregorio saw a person in the thick growth of manzanita, shrub brush, and mesquite trees. His eyes panned the area, but he saw only the immovable flora. Gregorio suspected the movement was the swimmer now on American soil. Gregorio had guessed right.

Gregorio continued his work. Out of the corner of his eye, he saw a man duck behind the shrub brush seconds later. Gregorio asked the man to come out from hiding. The man-in-hiding chose to speak from the cover of the large bush, stating he was naked, wearing only '*calzones*.'

Gregorio informed the hidden man he had seen men in their underwear before. He persuaded the man to come out by stating, "Don't make me look like a fool talking to a bush!"

Gregorio guessed the man's age to be the early twenties and about Gregorio's size, except for being relatively slender. (Gregorio was solidly built with an incredible physique.)

The young man sheepishly related he had bundled his shirt, trousers, and shoes and encircled them with his belt. The pack slipped away as he struggled with the current, failing to recover his clothing.

Gregorio assured the man he would correct his clothing dilemma, told him his name, and asked for his. *Agustín* was the young man's name. He still did not trust Gregorio and showed it when he meekly asked if Gregorio planned to report him to the "*Migra*"—border immigration personnel.

That question angered Gregorio, who forcibly retaliated, "Didn't I tell you I would get you clothes? I am Mexican, just like you. I came from *Jalisco, Guadalajara*. If you do not trust me, you can leave naked as you are."

Agustín lowered his head and profoundly begged forgiveness for his mistrust. *Agustín* came from the state of *Zacatecas*. He chose this area because *Agustín* had friends working in Harlingen, Texas, who had written promising him a job.

Agustín's meager funds ran out when he reached *Valle Hermoso, Tamaulipas. Agustín* walked from there to the *Río Bravo*, the Mexican name for the Río Grande—a two-day walk

For someone shy at first, *Agustín* was making up for it, which Gregorio enjoyed heartily showing with his hardy laugh, then let him know his wife, *María*, also came from the state of *Zacatecas*.

Gregorio removed his long-tailed shirt and handed it to *Agustín* with orders to put it on. Gregorio invited *Agustín* to his home, five minutes away, to eat the noon meal. Right off, *Agustín* turned down the invitation because he lacked pants. Gregorio let *Agustín* know he would remedy that by leaving *Agustín* behind when they came within eyesight of his home. *Agustín* could hide behind a bush while Gregorio fetched pants for him. (The entire area is covered with bushes and trees.)

During the meal, Gregorio weighed down *Agustín* with information about his behavior to not attract attention to himself, for *Agustín* became a *'wetback'*—subject to arrest—the moment he entered the United States.

After serving the meal, *María* retreated to get an extra set of clothes for *Agustín*. *María* carefully pinned two five-dollar bills and one ten inside the pants' pockets meant for *Agustín*.

María placed the clothes in a draw-string canvas bag and joined the men in the dining room. She was puzzled by the overwhelming advice Gregorio was giving *Agustín* and wondered if her husband was doing what the Río Grande failed to do—drown the poor fellow with an overload of information.

At the end of the meal, Gregorio presented *Agustín* with a pair of cowboy boots he rarely wore, a belt, and the hat Gregorio had been wearing. *Agustín* readily accepted the boots and buckled the belt while humbly declaring Gregorio should not give him his hat, but Gregorio would not accept no for an answer.

The couple shook hands with *Agustín*, wished him luck, and sent him on his way with these parting words, "Walk tall and proud; keep your head up!"

María turned, faced her husband, and hugged him softly, saying, "I love you, you crazy man."

DITCHING SCHOOL

Gregorio's children could not attend movies while living in Brownsville, Texas. The reasons the dad gave his children were: (1) it costs money, (2) you have evening chores concerning our animals, and (3) we do not own a car, and the bus does not run in this rural area.

Gregorio left out the MAIN reason: PREJUDICE! He knew much more about prejudice than his children since he was the one who encountered it most. Gregorio had always shielded his family from that ugly truth. Now that his children were older and would be capable of discerning it, he was not about to permit a head-on meeting on their own. *(The children attended Nogales School, where Mexicans outnumbered Whites 50 to one—this very remote school had only two white students.)*

Most of the older children had accepted their dad's explanation for not being permitted to attend theatres. His reasons were genuine and difficult to refute. Besides, in the 1950s, most theatres ran movies only on Friday night, started in the afternoon on Saturday, and never on Sunday.

Therefore, it is inexplicable why Gregorio's two oldest boys, José (Joe) and Rosalío (Ross), did what they did on this school day in 1955.

The boys and their older sister, Carmen, had just finished their sack lunches under one of the many *nogal* (walnut) trees on the school ground.

Pablo, a 17-year-old, drove his 1953 Dodge pickup right along the six-foot chain-link fence that enclosed the school property. Pablo whistled for Joe to join him at the fence.

Though Joe had only recently made friends with Pablo, he dashed to the boundary in a flash and motioned for Ross to join them.

Carmen raced after Ross, but her brothers had scaled the fence and entered Pablo's pickup before she could voice an objection. The boys heard Carmen's last, screamed warning, "You're in BIG TROUBLE!!!"

What had been Pablo's enticement? A FILM ABOUT GORILLAS!!! The brothers took the bait—a promise of a motion picture about gorillas! The year was 1955, so the world knew little about gorillas. That must have been why such a film was shown on a weekday. And the boys had minimal experience outside their highly pastoral, idyllic area in Cameron County. Their home was a stone's throw from the Rio Grande.

Joe, 13, and Ross, 11, did not recall anything about the film on gorillas. The stench of the *"Colored-only-balcony"* from where they had to watch the movie blocked any memory of the video. No one bothered to clean the only area Blacks and Mexicans were allowed.

The ditching school was an awakening experience with prejudice. Moreover, Gregorio soundly whipped his boys, and, of course, Joe and Ross did their chores in the dark.

Strangely, the poor juvenile delinquents did not mind the whipping; they knew they had it coming. The inhumanity they had endured that day overshadowed everything else. That was the only time they made mention of that incident to each other or anyone else.

Sixty-six years later, Joe denies this incident ever happened. Ross still can picture him and Joe running to the fence. He sees vividly the black and red Dodge pickup and Pablo standing by its driver's door. Other than that, Ross cannot recall a single image of the ride to Brownsville, the theatre, the film, the ride home, or the whipping!

SWIM THE RIO GRANDE

Far to the northwest, the young boy could see glimpses of lightning, but it was so far away he could not hear the thunderclaps. It was a Saturday morning in 1955.

The morning was much darker and overcast than Friday evening. The eleven-year-old boy could not see the Río Grande from his bedroom window, yet he could hear the water flow. His home was set on high ground, approximately 100 yards from the massive river in Brownsville, Texas's southernmost rural area.

The boy's father stated it had poured all Friday northwest from their location while sitting at supper the night before. He added the rain would be here Saturday morning. The father sent the boy early to bed, for he wanted him up before dawn Saturday.

The boy led the cow out for grazing right after she was milked. The man hoped the cow would graze for at least a few hours before the rain arrived. Thunder and lightning could be heard and seen.

The boy knew where he planned to allow the cow to graze. He wanted the cow across the river from gorgeous tennis courts on the Mexican side of the Río Grande. He hoped the club members would come despite the ugly weather.

Why did the boy wish for that when he knew nothing about tennis? Last week, his older brother informed him that the Mexican Club members' game was called '*tennis*.' That was all his brother's information. His brother did not know how it was played or about tennis.

The young lad was not interested in the game of tennis. He craved the beautiful white balls visible despite the courts' location--150 yards across from the American side of the river.

The boy had noticed balls often went through the chain-link fence and rolled among the brush that grew on the slopes of

Río Grande. He had planned to swim across the river as the river was at a low stage. Yes, there was a current, but it was slow, and the foolish boy thought himself a strong swimmer. He could manage such a current easily. Once on the Mexican side, he skimmed to sneak amongst the short brush, hide there, and wait for a stray tennis ball.

The boy was delighted when the tennis players arrived in fancy new cars. You could not ask for a better setting for these magnificent tennis courts. The view was pictorial, with greenery and the majestic river below. Visible bends at either side of the courts perfected the setting.

The foolish boy tethered the cow and swam across the Río Grande. It proved more tiring and complicated than he had thought, but he made it. That was the critical part. Everything was going as planned. He crawled or walked on his knees until he finally climbed the slope. (The boy did not want to be seen by the tennis players because he knew a boy his age retrieved the balls he planned to snatch.) The boy did not notice the thunder and lightning had stopped.

He could not hear the players' chatter or the balls' swatting. All he heard was the roar of the river, more noise than ten trains would have made. He stood up in time to see the cars leaving.

Where was the roaring noise coming from, if not the tennis courts? He turned around and saw a massive tidal wave of water; an enormous moving water wall came around the bend!

"OH, NO! OH, NO! OH, NO! He refused to believe what was right in front of him! The petrified boy thought if he denied it, the situation would disappear.

He had to face it; he was trapped on the wrong side of the Río Grande! *{The foolish boy was stranded on the river's side, known to Mexicans as Río Bravo.}*

The raging waters brought animals, trees, outhouses, chicken pens, the short brush which grew on the slopes, and everything else you could imagine. The nightmare was made worse as the sky opened and poured rain so heavy the boy could not see the American side of the swollen river. He was doomed! WHY? WHY? WHY? Had he been so STUPID?

His father always told him, "Do not swim in the river, much less try to swim across it. I know you. You are always attempting the impossible. At most, you may wash your hands at the river's edge. BUT NEVER, NEVER, NEVER PUT YOUR WHOLE BODY IN THE RIVER!"

The ignorant boy had defied his father again. And, this time, he might have to pay with his life. (Would his corpse be found at the mouth of the river which empties into the Gulf of Mexico?) He shuddered at that thought and quickly put it out of his mind.)

The boy's profound sorrow caused him to start crying, but he immediately stopped when he saw his father on the American side of the Río Grande. His mother stood next to her husband, but only for a second. She fainted when she saw her baby on the Mexican side of the river.

His father was trying to scream instructions to him, waving his hands wildly, but the resounding, persistent noise made it impossible to hear even one word.

Encouraged now that he saw his father, the boy watched the torrent, hoping against hope that it would slow down. It did not. Yet, there was hope for the boy. There was not as much debris embroiled in the speeding water.

The Río Grande had elevated to the top of the banks—at least three times the water it carried when the boy swam across. Worse yet, the water was rushing, not meandering as before! The boy took a deep breath and plunged into the tumultuous river. When the boy came up, he stroked with all his might. It was tempting to swim underwater, not to see the debris, but the boy dared not. He noted how the muddy, murky water made it impossible to see anything when he dove. A large piece of junk could knock him unconscious or confine him underwater.

The hellish current was taking the boy downriver rapidly. Occasionally, he had to dodge debris, which only complicated his swim across the mighty, wild river.

A rope came to him when he thought he could swim no more! Smartly, his father had run along the bank and ahead of the boy to toss the cow's 100-foot rope and perhaps reach his son.

The boy grabbed the rope and did not let go as his father pulled and pulled and pulled until his son was safe on the American side.

SAND IN MY SOUP

Plainview, Texas, provided the worst cotton crop of the four places the family had picked cotton in the harvest of 1955. The top choice was a close race between El Campo, Texas, and Lubbock, Texas. Though in third best, Temple's cotton yield was superior to Plainview's cotton output.

Worse yet, Plainview was nearly the death of the family or at least some of the family!

The farmer hurriedly pulled the family out of his cotton field and into the meager shack he offered the family, picking his cotton. A horrendous dust storm was approaching rapidly! The farmer's wife supplied the family with sheets to cut into strips. The couple then demonstrated how to pack every open gap in the shack with strips of cloth by using the blade section of butter knives.

While the family plugged the openings, the father and the middle-aged farmer boarded the windows in the shack. In the meantime, the farmer's wife hurried home to bring back candles for the family to use during the dust storm.

The family did not appreciate this until the storm hit the small farm less than an hour later. The shack would have been pitch black had it not been for the candles. More critical, had the family not filled the cracks in the shack, they could have choked to death on the dust and sand!

As it was, the family was terrified! They had never even come close to experiencing something like this blinding dust storm. The parents struggled to keep a false front, for they would panic the children much more if they appeared scared.

The father told stories, and the mother prepared chicken soup. They strived to keep their routine, thus keeping the youngsters at ease.

When the soup was ready, the family sat at the table and endeavored to have a typical meal. Minutes into the meal, the oldest boy attempted to blurt out, "There is *sand in my soup*!" Only in

mid-sentence, the father interrupted by finishing his sentence, "...SALT in the soup."

He explained, "There is supposed to be salt in the soup. Otherwise, there is no taste in it. Eat it before it gets cold." All the while, the father intently looked at the boy so that he got the message. Nothing more was said about the "*sand in the soup.*"

The mother washed the bowls once the meal was finished. Meantime, the father continued telling stories. The dust storm was relentless—raging on and on for hours. Its eerie sound was all around.

Soon the children commenced falling asleep. The father ordered them to bed, but the mother did not allow her children to lay down for the night unless they washed their faces and brushed their teeth first. The father saw her reasoning since everyone in the shack wore a chalky off-white face and arms from the superfine dust that infiltrated the shack. Dusty faces occurred despite the large handkerchief each child had worn over their nose and mouth.

With the children asleep, the parents could speak openly without fear of being heard by the youngsters. The father worried about what the fierce, blowing sand would do to the scanty cotton crop. The mother agonized about the health effects of dust and sand on the children.

Next, the mother questioned, "Snow in Lubbock! Dust storm here! Are these incidents telling us to go home—Brownsville? Already, the children have lost three months of schooling."

The father did not intend to return, "It was snowing when we left Lubbock. I don't believe our vehicle can make it in the snow and, by now, even ice! Have you forgotten? It is December!"

An argument ensued, with the mother blaming the father for migrating this far away from the safety of their home, thus putting the entire family at risk. She called attention to the obvious—the fierce dust storm and their unsafe, insecure shack. Next, she mentioned their difficulty in the snow when leaving Lubbock.

The father defended himself by saying he was not responsible for Lubbock's snow or Plainview's horrific dust storm. He said that such things happen no matter where they live. He pointed out the poor conditions in Mexico before they came to America. Along with the deplorable living, there was frightening thunder and lightning, flooding, and rain damage. He dramatically recalled the death of their cows due to lightning.

The mother said they had never faced such misfortunes in their eight years in Brownsville. Sure, they were fearful during the hurricane season, but the most they received was heavy rain and stiff wind. They easily tolerated those results.

The back-and-forth bickering abruptly stopped when the couple realized all was quiet—the dust storm had ended! The parents washed their faces and went to bed.

The farmer came to the shack early morning to check on his workers. Instead, he found the father in the cotton field. Mesmerized, the father stood in a field of bent, bare cotton stalks. Just the central stalk survived the sand. There was not one single ball of cotton visible.

The farmer inquired about the family's welfare, especially the children. He was pleased they were all fine. He strongly suggested the father make sure his children drank water all day. They needed to wash the dust and sand out of their system.

Before the farmer left, he added that the family could stay in his cabin until they decided what to do next.

Once confident, standing tall, the father appearing much older than his thirty years, walked through the door, wearing a wholly lost look, and announced, "The cotton is all gone! We will be moving again, but we don't know where or when this time!"

"INDIAN COTTON"

The migrant family was on their second day of traveling through Arizona. Arkansas was their home state, but they didn't return home to Trumann this time after picking cotton in El Campo, Texas, and Lubbock, Texas. The family of seven decided they were going to California. Charlie Watson had heard beautiful things about California and was determined to see for himself.

Bennie Sue, Charlie's wife, agreed; she was anxious for a better place for her five children—three boys and two girls— ages were equally spaced two years apart. The children, of course, delighted in going to a new place. The season was autumn, the year 1953.

Doyle, the eldest youngster, was driving. Doyle was just sixteen yet had been driving since he was fourteen. As the family's vehicle approached Eloy, Arizona, Charlie shot straight up, banging his head on the car's roof! He yelled at Doyle to stop.

Charlie's sudden excitement startled Doyle, so he slammed on the brakes. Charlie hustled out of the car and made a Bee-line for the tallest cotton plants he had seen in his cotton-picking days in Arkansas and Texas.

Charlie gently touched the fluffy white stuff and joyfully screamed, "IT IS COTTON!" Except for Doyle, the rest of the brood ran into the tall cotton plants. Bennie Sue yelled for the children to come out of the "white jungle."

Charlie laughed loudly—more cotton for his family to pick. They were short on funds and welcomed the chance to earn money to cover expenses for the rest of the trek to California.

Bennie Sue eyed a small patch of trees and asked Doyle to drive there so she could prepare baloney sandwiches for the family.

Only the children were still eating when an old pickup driven by an older man pulled up next to them. The gentleman walked straight to Charlie and extended his hand in a friendly manner.

The man introduced himself as Jimmy Wilson. He proudly said this cotton was his and asked would Charlie's family be interested in harvesting it for him. The pay-per-pound was higher than the Watson family had ever been paid.

Charlie did not answer immediately; instead, he declared that his family had picked cotton in his native Arkansas and Texas, but never had they seen such tall cotton. Charlie asked why this cotton was so late since it was late fall.

The courteous, refined man stated his cotton was called "*Pima*." He added that it was named after an Indian tribe who inhabited this territory centuries ago. Jimmy proudly retorted that Arizona grew crops slightly different from Arkansas and Texas. He said irrigation and a long growing season made as many as three crops possible yearly.

Charlie recalled Jimmy Wilson's question about picking this cotton and answered he would have to discuss it with his wife and children first.

Mr. Wilson motioned to a group of buildings about a quarter of a mile away. He said Charlie's family was welcome to use the facilities there for rest, freshen up, wash clothes, whatever with no obligation. If the Watsons decided to pick his cotton, they should pick one of the three cabins as their home.

Jimmy then pointed in the opposite direction at his home and told Charlie to come to notify him about their decision.

Bennie Sue investigated the cabins carefully, for she knew Charlie and was confident they would pick this *"Indian"* cotton. Bennie Sue was beside herself, for the cabins had running cold and hot water inside and electricity! These benefits were nonexistent when they picked cotton in Arkansas and Texas.

Things were certainly looking better and better! The Watsons could hardly wait to get to California. What surprises awaited them there?

But first, they had to pick this "Indian cotton."

TOMMY WALKS ALONE

Lawanna Rudd was not surprised when someone knocked at her back door. She clutched her purse, which she had kept close at hand since returning from the bank hours earlier. A widow, Mrs. Rudd paused as if praying with both hands in the interior of her purse. She arranged her purse over her neck and under her left arm, and only then did Lawanna boldly answer the door.

Her only grandson, Tommy, was at the door. He looked much older than his 38 years.

"Hello, Tommy! Come in! Come in! Do not stand there in the rain. I was half-expecting you late last night. How have you been? Are you thirsty? Hungry? No, wait, your phrase for being hungry was, '*My tummy is fighting with my back*!' Do you still say that when you are hungry? Look at me! I have not given you a chance to speak. Take a seat in the dining room. I will get you a drink, then heat something to satisfy your tummy. Go on! Go on!"

Tommy did not bother with his Nan's questions. "If it is all the same with you, Nan, I'll stay with you. I have already pulled out your phone line but I still don't trust you. You are too righteous." Tommy's words were biting. He attempted to take control of the situation.

Unfazed, Nan opened the refrigerator and drew out a pitcher of tea. She turned and stepped to reach into the cupboard for a large glass. "Put in your ice, Tommy," Nan told Tommy, handing him the glass. Her tone was firm, giving the message she was not releasing control.

Tommy loaded his glass with crushed ice and faced Nan. She poured the tea.

"You know where the sugar is, Tommy. Help yourself." Again, Nan was demonstrative.

"How did you know I would come here? Why were you expecting me last night? Tommy's voice was gruff and demeaning, always seeking to be dominant.

Nan answered, "Your escape from the prisoner-transport van has been constant news. Reports stated you were likely in this area—warning the usual, '*may be armed and dangerous.*' And I am your only family still living in the county. I was sure you would wait until you thought it safe to come. I suppose you think the light rain and poor visibility favor you. The police were here last night and returned this morning."

Nan talked as she served Tommy a plate of food. "Where did you get those clothes? You snatched them from a clothesline, would be my guess. Oh, Tommy, I hope you have not hurt anyone since your escape.

"I have not forgotten how much you love potato salad and deviled eggs, Tommy. I have a fresh German chocolate cake, your favorite, for dessert. I made your food this morning."

"What did you tell them?" Tommy asked in a cross-tone before starting on the food like a starving junk-yard dog.

Lawanna's attention had been on Tommy's stomach, so she questioned, "Tell who?"

"THE COPS! FIVE-0! THE PIGS!" Tommy shot back, angry and frustrated the cops knew where to look for him.

"Tommy, I sure wish you would not be so disrespectful, especially in my home! I told the truth, Tommy. I was not about to lie for you—not to the officers. I let them know I had not had contact with you. I could tell the officers doubted me, so I insisted they search every inch of my home and garage, which they politely did. I suspect they are watching the house even as we speak and will come knocking once it gets dark."

"DON'T BET ON THAT! It is raining hard now, and the Pigs do not like to get wet. They might melt. Nan, you have never liked me! Why?" Tommy's tone said he was feeling sorry for himself.

"That is where you are dead wrong, son," Retorted Nan.

"DON'T CALL ME, SON! I am not your son. I am not anybody's son. My dad disowned me. Maybe I had a mother, but she, too, abandoned me. She ran off with another man. So, you see, I do not belong to anybody. I am all alone." Tommy was openly crying—an implicit declaration saying he was right, but everyone else was WRONG!

"Please, Tommy, listen for a moment. Would you, please? Sweetie, we all deeply loved you. Maybe we love you too much. My son was ecstatic! He got the boy he wanted so badly. We all prayed for a boy. Did we spoil you? Absolutely! But we also loved and cherished your sister when she came along. You were jealous of the love we showed your baby sister. You were selfish. You wanted to be the only one. Tommy, you were mean to her. Eventually, your jealousy turned to hostility. Tommy, she was your little sister, five years younger than you."

"Go ahead, Nan, blame me for COVID, too! Why not?" Tommy angrily interrupted.

"I am not here for a lecture. I came for a gun and money. Now, give!"

Despite Tommy's anger, Nan kept calm. "I do not own a gun. As you recall, you STOLE Papa's gun. A gun is unnecessary in this home, so I did not replace it. I carry very little money and FROZE my bank accounts this morning. Food and drink, I will give you. You are welcome to Papa's clothes; they will fit you. Other than that, I have only advice to give you.

"Let me continue, Tommy. The family did not love you any less after your sister's birth. But heaven knows why; you saw it that way. Tommy, you kept getting worse and worse. As you grew older, so did your wrath—by leaps and bounds!

"Your mother did not see it that way at first. She was unyielding in your defense. Your poor mother figured you would outgrow your badness.

"The rest of the family attempted to channel your desires, emotions, and feeling in the right direction to no avail. Instead, you chose hostility, strife, and jealousy as your companions.

"Did we fail you, Tommy? No, your sister picked up on those virtues, plus love, kindness, and compassion—ethics you lacked and rejected.

"Tommy, you consistently chose the wrong things to do. You picked the wrong entertainment and friends and showed no respect for elders or authority. You lacked self-discipline and discernment. Tommy, you say you are nobody's son, yet, your behavior has been that of the Devil's own."

"What do you know about that? You have never suffered; you have never lacked for anything. Look at this house," screamed Tommy. He raised out of his seat and added, "Now, are you going to get me a gun?"

"Tommy, I already answered that! Do not go there again. Your time is running out. If you want to blame somebody, blame your poor mother—poor soul! By forever shielding you, she was enabling you.

"May he rest in peace; your father was a loving dad. He kindly tried to correct you. But you, Tommy, slapped his helping hand away. He introduced you to team sports—and bought you a nice expensive baseball glove. You refused to play *'catch'* with him.

"He and Papa built you an excellent basketball standard. You refused to shoot baskets with your dad. Then, you, Tommy, were furious at him for shooting baskets with the neighborhood kids and teaching them the game. One night, you destroyed the standard!

"Your dad bailed you out of trouble time and again. He paid for costly legal fees, recovery programs, and counseling that you invariably quit or turned down altogether. Your dad, Tommy, would not give up on you when everyone else, including me, did."

"Lies! Lies! Lies! Dad did give up on me. He told me so himself!" Tommy screamed in anger.

"Tommy, I am sorry; forgive me! Yes, you are correct; you are right, Tommy. It was painful; I want to forget when my son came to me in tears right after hearing you killed a man. I felt so sorry for my son; he looked pitiful and lost. You, Tommy, had brought him to his knees. Between sobs and his face awash with tears, your father chose his words carefully, *'I have gone as far as I can with Tommy. From now on, Tommy walks alone.'*

"So do not dare blame my son for giving up on you! Tommy, you had just taken a man's life! I will forever blame you for my son's premature death and the death of my beloved Papa. Your insistence on leading a life of crime killed them!"

"Nan, not even the justice system gave up on me! But my flesh and blood did. The courts always let me off due to *insufficient evidence, no witnesses*, or *a legal mistake*. But you, Nan, have no loopholes, no forgiveness!"

"Tommy, you view the justice system as STUPID and firmly suppose it gave you LICENSE to continue your criminal ways. Tommy, I am NOT the justice system! For once, Tommy, do the right thing. Turn yourself in!" As Mrs. Lawanna Rudd spoke, she walked to the front door.

Cold with hate for the whole world, Tommy crossed his arms in defiance. But Tommy quickly changed his demeanor and pleaded, "Nan, please, please, give me the keys to your car; I have got to get away! They are going to give me the *needle!*"

"Tommy, no keys, no car! I never believed in the *death penalty* before you took a life. I was not ever directly associated with capital punishment. But now, I see it as the only way to keep you from taking another life. If God disagrees with my thinking, may He severely punish me. I feel for you; I honestly do. Yet, it would be best to be held accountable for all your wrongdoing, particularly for the lives you have taken."

Tommy defended his actions, "Nan, those people gave me no choice. That was not on me!"

"Tommy, I love you but hate what you have done. I am doing the hardest thing I have ever had to do. I am doing it for your father, mother, Papa, and sister."

"Nan, what are you saying? Spit it out straight!"

"Tommy, you no doubt think I keep my purse hanging from my shoulder, so you won't steal from me as you have in the past," Mrs. Rudd stated while looking through the front door's peephole.

"Tommy, if that is what you thought, you are mistaken! My purse contains a cell phone which is connected to the police. They have heard every word you and I have spoken. Tommy, you can be sure officers are stationed at every window and door. DO NOT try anything that will get you killed in my presence, please, Tommy!" Finished, Mrs. Lawanna Rudd opened the front door for the police.

JELLY BELLIES

The older man visited the bathroom and walked a short walk. The man's rest stop was over. Yes, he was hungry and tired. The oldster was delighted, for he was going to see his granddaughter for only the second time. Slowly, the man walked back to his bus.

The man saw his granddaughter four years earlier on the day of her birth. After the aged man's granddaughter was born, he had to hurry home to arrange his wife's funeral. The man's beloved wife of forty years passed away the day before his granddaughter's birth. *{The man's emotions were gnarled. He was thrilled because his daughter had given birth just before her child-bearing age expired. Yet, he was tormented that his dear wife had not witnessed that. Thus began the man's most critical episode in his life!}*

For four years following the old gentleman's wife's death, he had been in a cloud of profound sadness. The man's depression had hospitalized him more than once. It had been six months since his last *"black-hole"* episode, his most extended time without a debilitating dark period. The aging man felt he was finally ready to see his only grandchild.

The aged man returned to his seat at the front of the bus. He had just made himself comfortable a distinguished lady about his age stopped beside him. She held the hand of a delightful little girl. She kindly asked the gray man if he would care for her granddaughter. The lady informed the man the child's name was Hannah, and she was four years old. She also asked that he ensure Hannah got off the bus at Glen Oaks. Hanna's mother would be there to meet her.

The charming lady was the mother of Hannah's father. She was a new face to the aged man. Likewise, the lady had no recollection of seeing the older man before. Perfect strangers? Even though the age-old gentleman was tired and hungry, he readily agreed to take excellent care of Hannah. He promised to treat her as his granddaughter and added he was going to Glen Oaks to visit his granddaughter.

The attractive lady smiled happily and handed him Hannah's colorful overnight bag. As the distinguished man took hold of the overnight bag, he gave the friendly lady his best smile and wisely asked for the lady's phone number. The man said it was just in case anything went wrong, yet, he liked her smile and how she made him feel--like his dear, departed wife.

Hannah's grandma asked for the man's phone number, agreeing with his request. She, too, added, *"Just in case!"*

The bus started to move, and Hannah and the man waved goodbye to Hannah's grandmother. They both made themselves comfortable, for they had a two-hour bus ride.

Now relaxed, the poor man's stomach complained, letting him know it was empty and wanted something to fill it. He ate a light breakfast at 5 a.m. and nothing since then. It was now 6 p.m. The man had been riding the bus since 7 a.m. Due to his medical condition, he was not allowed to drive.

Hannah heard the hungry stomach growling for food, so she asked if he had anything to feed his tummy. Embarrassed, the man heavily shook his head no. {*The man had used up all his savings on hospital expenses. He had just enough for a round-trip bus ticket and a darling, expensive music box the man brought for his grandchild. He knew his daughter would care for his needs while visiting and prepare a lunch bag for his return trip. Once back at his home, a Social Security check should be in his mail.}*

Hannah opened her *"going-to-Nana"* bag and took out a package of *"jelly bellies."* She offered to share them with the hungry man because she wanted to feed the belly, begging for something to eat.

All the rest of the trip, Hannah helped fill the empty tummy. While eating *"jelly bellies,"* the grateful man and Hannah visited. He told Hannah his wife had passed away just before the birth of his granddaughter, the one he was going to visit. His wife was Hannah, so their daughter and son-in-law named their baby Hannah in her honor.

The dear man told Hannah he had not seen his granddaughter since birth. He let Hannah know his granddaughter was four years old, just like her.

Hannah said, "My name is Hannah, and I am four!"

The sweet man answered, "What are the chances of that? You also live in Glen Oaks, just like my Hannah! I would very much like for you to meet my Hannah. You might become best friends."

Hannah was polite and very good at holding a conversation, especially considering she was only four years old. Hannah told her new friend she had been visiting her Nana because she was sad. {*The anniversary of Nana's husband's death had caused her deep sadness, but Hannah only knew that she had been sent to visit Nana and make her happy.*}

Hannah loved her Nana, but she could not stay any longer, as her other grandpa, whom she had never met, was coming to visit her.

They talked and ate *"jelly bellies"*; then ate *"jelly bellies"* and talked. When the man asked Hannah her mother's name, she said it was "Mommy," but Daddy called her "Honey, Sugar, and Baby."

The dear man's stomach no longer made growling noises. The time went by quickly. Before they realized it, the bus pulled into Glen Oaks.

The sweet little man walked Hannah off the bus to find her mother. Once outside, he placed her high on his shoulders because the older gentleman had gotten so attached to Hannah and wanted Hannah to be up high so her mother could spot her in the crowd.

The older man and Hannah were startled to hear a loud, surprised shriek!

They saw a lovely young woman with both hands over her mouth as they faced the direction of the scream.

The woman was Hannah's mother and the man's daughter!

ON MY WAY TO SAN JOSE

The hitchhiker quickened his pace. He was headed west on this lonely, flat California Highway 152. It had been some miles since his last ride, and it was getting late, though he could not tell the time since he did not own a watch. He did not own a car, either. Truth be known, his only possession of any value were his hands. These same hands were now his most significant concern.

He was on his way to San José. Tonight, he would be fighting the most crucial fight of his young, promising boxing career as a light heavyweight. The prizefighter was only 19, was 5'10", 175 pounds, and looked like a renowned sculptor had chiseled him out of granite. His short brown hair and clean-shaven face gave him a handsome look.   He had been boxing professionally for 13 months and was already at a crossroads.

He was in outstanding physical condition. The few miles he had to walk between rides after leaving his home in Fresno were nothing compared to the daily roadwork he did as part of his training. Four to 6 miles were not taxing to him in the least. He did hundreds of sit-ups, push-ups, and pull-ups daily, including Saturdays and Sundays. If cornered to be truthful, he would confess his three favorite components: the speed bag, the rope jumping, and the sparring. His powerful blows came from lifting weights an hour every other day, and the impact speed of his punches—was slightly over 20 mph.

All, except the young man, believed he carried his training to excess. His focus was on his mom and two sisters. He longed to get them out of the world of poverty. Just as intense was his passion for boxing; he loved the training part just as much as the actual boxing. Boxing people constantly reminded him about his immense abilities, which were limitless.

His hands were lightning-fast and dealt brutal blows all over his opponent's body. People with extensive boxing knowledge said he was a '*natural*,' '*born to box,*' '*one in a million,* '*would go far,*' *etc.*

Whoever dared get in the ring with him did so only once, for the foe was dealt such punishment; he had no ambition for a rematch. The damage his fists administered was the reason for the hitchhiker's torment. He had put his last two opponents in the hospital, one in a coma, which greatly unnerved him.

{*This was probably due to concussions, which at that time—1959-- were known as dementia pugilistic, meaning "insane boxer." In 1959 concussions were not readily diagnosed. Thus, the boxer was referred to as "punchy," "goofy," "coo-coo," and "punch-drunk."*}

For a good reason, the slugger was called "Iron Fists," which fit Isaac's first name and last name Irons—Isaac "Iron Fists" Irons. Isaac detested the moniker, but the *Fresno Bee* and the San José *Mercury News* had stuck him with it.

Isaac's major bouts occurred in the San José Arena, but he trained in Fresno and fought lesser fights there.

Isaac guessed he was less than ten miles from Los Baños, and if correct, he had covered only 60 miles—less than half of the 150 miles from Fresno to San José.

Irons wished he had started his trek hours earlier, but it was too late. No need to worry about what should have been—he had other things bothering him. Isaac had already missed his pre-fight medical examination and his weigh-in.

A car slowed down and stopped next to Isaac, and the driver asked him if he wanted a ride. Without a word, Isaac answered by quickly climbing into the car.

The driver introduced himself as Arthur Fowler. His grey temples gave evidence of his wisdom, education, and age. Mr. Fowler told Isaac to toss his duffel bag on the back seat and grab something to drink from the ice chest behind him on the floorboard.

While Isaac was busy doing that, Arthur asked his name and added, "I'm on my way to San José. I can give you a lift that far. If your destination is San Francisco, you are out of luck. I will visit my parents and do maintenance work this weekend."

Isaac related his story between drinks of water: "My name is Isaac Irons. Fresno is my home. I am on my way to San José. I appreciate you stopping for me. I am a prizefighter on the card as the main event at 9—my first main event. I have already missed my medical check-up and weigh-in, but with your help, I should make it in time for my bout. I have been late since I do not have a car, a trainer, or a sponsor. I do not trust anybody in boxing, not even myself. The promoter, Mr. Farley, will be furious at me. He has a terrible temper."

"I am from Selma. We are practically neighbors. I am a high school counselor. With all your walking, won't your legs be too tired for your match?" Asked Fowler.

"A boxer's legs are crucial, especially if the fight lasts ten rounds. Mine never do. I always have the good fortune to knock out my opponent in three rounds or less—seven fights, 7 KOs. Opponents say my punches have that special "*sting*" to them, as if charged with electricity—they hurt so.

"I am fearful my fists are becoming more and more lethal—that is why I don't trust myself. My last two fights ended horribly for my opponents. I am terrified I might kill somebody in the ring or put him in a coma from which he will never return.

"But I know nothing else. I started boxing at age nine, and that is all I know. I never even finished high school because I wanted to help Mom with money. My father deserted us when I was four. By the time I was 16, I had been a '*gym rat*' for seven years—

working and training, waiting for the day I would box with a purpose behind it. I had sparred with numerous fighters, some well-known, and I more than held my own against them.

"People believe I carry my training too far. I am afraid I have to disagree. I want to be like Rocky Marciano and retire as an undefeated champion! I have never lost a fight, not even in Golden Gloves, which I started at age 16, just before quitting school. So far, no fighter has hurt me, much less sent me to the canvass. Men with boxing know-how say I am a *'natural'*— *'one-in-a-million.'* I consider myself blessed."

After a short silence, the counselor said, "What I know about boxing would fit in a coffee cup, but I know people and how to counsel. You are very wise to be concerned for others. That is admirable and very human; other boxers delight in punishing their foes. Perhaps, if someone charted your foes so they were equal to your talents, you would be less likely to do severe damage.

"If that is not possible, you could keep your job at the gym and make yourself available to spar with other boxers—surely, sparring partners get paid. Undoubtedly, there is always a need for sparring mates. And, since a boxer, while sparring, uses headgear, your blows would not be as damaging. At the same time, this would

sustain your intense love for boxing, and you would have the

pleasure of defeating boxers that perhaps no one else could. You

are still young; I suggest you finish high school through night

classes. I hope you find a solution; I am confident you will. If you

are even a bit religious, pray about your dilemma."

Mr. Arthur Fowler dropped Isaac at the boxer's entrance to the San

José Arena, where a teenager, whom Isaac recognized as Dennis,

was waiting for him right next to the payphone.

 The teen told Isaac that Mr. Farley did not want to see his face

again. Farley had replaced Isaac, and he would be arrested and

charged with trespassing if he entered the arena.

Isaac did not seem to be paying attention to what Dennis was

saying. His concentration was on the boy's split lip and dried

blood.

"Did Farley do this?" He asked as he gently lifted Dennis's chin.

The teen just hung his head in stony silence.

Isaac ordered Dennis to walk along as he walked toward Farley's

office. The boy lagged and pleaded, "Please forget, Isaac! It will just cause more trouble! Farley told me to keep my mouth shut. I am fine; it will be gone by morning. He will have you arrested. Farley said you could not touch him. You are a professional boxer; your fists are weapons. And besides, he is much bigger than you, and if you cannot fight back, he will hurt you! Please, please, Isaac, leave it alone! Do not make trouble, Isaac!!!"

{Farley was 6'3" and weighed about 250 pounds, with a vicious temper to match that physique.}

Isaac walked faster and, without looking back, told Dennis to walk with him and not speak unless he asked him to.

Two arena cops were on either side of Farley's office door. Isaac told the one to his left to inform Doc he had arrived for his physical. He asked the cop on his right to call the boy's parents. That cop immediately stood up and reached for the door handle. Isaac spoke firmly, "No! Use the pay phone at the arena entrance. Doc will be busy here."

Isaac, with Dennis in tow, walked into Farley's office. Farley sprung from his desk and yelled, "You are not supposed to be here! Get the hell out!!!"

Isaac turned and locked the door. "First things first!" Isaac exclaimed, "Since when have you started beating up on innocent boys?"

His fists moved so quickly that Farley did not realize he had been hit in the stomach until he was on the floor in pain.

"Get up, Tub of lard!!! Get up, so I can send you down again!"

"You are in deep trouble! You used your fists on me! You are the one who is going down!" Farley whimpered as he slowly got up, thinking his words had hit home.

Like a flash, Isaac used Farley's stomach as a punching bag. Again, Farley hit the floor. And, again, Isaac ordered Farley to stand up and take his beating like a man.

This time Farley said nothing. You could see the fear in his eyes. Yet, he refused to get up. When Isaac threatened to stomp him to death, thoroughly beaten, Farley raised.

Isaac feigned his fists at Farley's stomach, stopped, and said, "Oh, hell!"

He landed a combination on Farley's face, and down he went like a lead balloon. Farley was down for the count, and blood was oozing from a cut above his left eye.

With Dennis behind, Isaac unlocked the door and walked out just in time to meet Doc.

With authority, Isaac told Doc, "Quick! Tend to Mr. Farley! He jumped out of his desk in rage, slipped, and hit his face on the corner of his desk. He is out cold and has a nasty cut over an eye! Dennis saw it all, right Dennis?"

"It happened just like Isaac said. It scared the heebie-jeebies out of me—all that blood!!!" Exclaimed Dennis with teenage glee.

As Doc rushed in to see after Farley, the other cop came and told Isaac Dennis' parents would pick him up within minutes. He was to wait for them at the pay phone.

Isaac put his right arm across Dennis' shoulders as they walked out of the arena forever.

BLACKIE: KING OF THE CANINES

Mostly Lab, Blackie was typical at birth, but Blackie grew more imposing and muscular than normal Labs. A lot had to do with his early life, for he loved to play rough and tough with his brothers! But more evident was the life Blackie led. It needs to be said Blackie was far removed from the average canine.

Blackie's age was unknown when he refused to cower to an older, more prominent, and experienced dog. Blackie may have lost the fight, but the Alpha dog backed off. Blackie cataloged all the moves of the highly reputed dog.

Days later, Blackie was neither afraid nor surprised when another dog attacked him. Not a minute into the fight, the attacker acknowledged his foolishness and, tail between his legs hurried off-- an embarrassing defeat.

Not by choice, Blackie's lifelong career as the top dog had started—Blackie: King of the Canines!

These encounters with a distinguished dog larger than Blackie brought him to the limelight. Before these bouts, no one recalled laying eyes on Blackie. Did he have an owner? Where was Blackie's home?

Blackie and his three brothers plus one sister had been deposited in the desert by a cowardly person when they were two months old.

Disappointed the puppies were not purebred, the despicable man took the coward's way out when distinctive features became apparent. The selfish man had paid dearly to have his purebred female bred by a champion, but apparently, another dog had gotten to her.

Not soon enough to save his sister and most petite brother, Blackie found the water to irrigate the cotton and alfalfa fields bordering the desert. Blackie and his two remaining brothers survived on grasshoppers, crickets, lizards, and other small critters.

Kit foxes also coveted the water, and coyotes quenched their thirst there.

Kit foxes posed a problem only for a few weeks. The puppies got larger quickly, and with Blackie's leadership, they fended off the foxes relatively easily.

The coyotes posed a more significant threat. Blackie educated his brothers on how to fight off small groups. The three brothers wisely learned to avoid large packs.

Even so, Blackie's brothers fell short of their first birthday. While sharing a giant jackrabbit, a pack of coyotes desired their food. Blackie fought ferociously yet tactically. Blackie ran them off by demolishing two vermin, but by then, the coyotes had done away with Blackie's siblings. The death of his brothers was a heavy weight on Blackie. Inadequacy and grief clawed at his heart.

After that attack, the coyotes knew to leave Blackie alone unless they were in groups of a dozen or more. Blackie was too big, too dangerous, and too wise a fighter. Besides, coyotes are cowards!

Months passed, and water became a dire problem since the crops were no longer irrigated.

 Blackie departed the desert and cotton/alfalfa fields. He needed another water source, and he longed for companionship. He came upon a small village not far from what had long been his source of food—rabbits, jackrabbits, and pheasants. Yes, Blackie was that quick!

Blackie visited the village only for water. He became increasingly robust and an expert at moves that made his opponents flee for their lives. Coyotes dared confront Blackie only when they were starving and easily outnumbered him— wishing Blackie to flee and leave them his food.

By now, Blackie was a seasoned fighter, yet not *one* scrimmage did he initiate. Blackie respected all living things and wanted the same. He understood his environment and the complexity of surviving it without wasting energy on needless conflicts.

Blackie roamed far and wide, perhaps searching for companionship, a human home, or both. Blackie could not "buy" a friend, so he remained a loner and lived free of responsibilities—to do what he loved.

Nonetheless, because of Blackie's first two dog fights, owners of dogs were quick to *'sic'em'* against Blackie when they spotted him.

That, of course, was a huge mistake. The glory-seeking owners' dogs were easy prey for Blackie, who seemed to have a "game plan" far beyond what any mongrel dog knew.

As Blackie matured, he became frustrated at owners turning their dogs on him when he only wanted to be left alone to roam and hunt for food.

Blackie employed a move in which he, quick as a cat, rammed the area of his attacker between the head and shoulder and, simultaneously, swept the opposite front paw. This move flipped his opponent on its back. Lightning fast, Blackie would clasp his teeth on his foe's throat and fling him back— an instant killing move.

One would think Blackie's reputation would deter other dog owners from risking their dogs, but the opposite was true. More and more born-fool owners wished their dog to be the one who dethroned Blackie.

Blackie certainly was not conscious of that. He had long reasoned to end these attacks by killing a dog or two, thus discouraging dog owners from risking their dogs. (Common, Blackie was *not!*)

Black as coal, with a slick, shiny coat Blackie went on safaris four-mile radius of his water source. Like a proud black stallion, the beautiful stride told all dogs, *"...keep away!"* Did Blackie have a queen? A prince? Or a princess? No one knew. Blackie was as mysterious as the night. There have been other dogs like Blackie, but only in comic books!

Sadly, an old fool will never listen or see what is plainly in sight. Such a fool noticed Blackie approaching his hometown. Had Blackie visited a village four miles away? Or was he returning from a roaming/hunting trip?

At any rate, the ignoramus immediately sent his dog against the tired, thirsty, but still strong Blackie.

Frustrated, Blackie killed the idiot's dog instantly. Blackie resumed his quest for water. Numerous shoppers at the grocery store and gas station witnessed Blackie's quick kill. These witnesses also knew the feebleminded fool who stupidly sent his dog to death. He was the meanest, most hated man in town. The witnesses all agreed Blackie's days were numbered!

Sure enough, the demon-possessed crackpot went home, got his rifle, and overflowed the small cavity in front of the public water faucet behind the businesses.

The detestable man hid and made ready.

Not having found water at any of his other known places, and smelling water at the public faucet, Blackie, tired, dehydrated, and remorseful at having killed another dog, approached the slight depression of water. Blackie smelled trouble an instant too late.

It took a loony and a rifle to dethrone the King of the Canines!

TWELVE HOURS TO LIVE

The youngest one (not yet 20) was named Ignacio ("Nacho.")
Ernesto, 24, was better known as "Orejón." Orejón means
"one with large ears" in Spanish--the equivalent in English is
calling a person with large ears "Dumbo." The oldest, at 25,
answered to "Pancho," yet his given name was Francisco.
DEAD! All three had just joined the departed! These three
had been riding in the back seat of the late-model Cadillac.
The three in the front seat were dead as well.

The lifeless bodies were scattered in an area about the size of
a house lot. The late-model Cadillac Sedan Deville did not
resemble the beautiful, cream-colored car it had been just
seconds before. The clock in the Cadillac stopped at 12:42
P.M.

Even the California Highway Patrolman could not believe it, and it had been his misfortune to witness this tragic accident. He was in shock. He was overwhelmed by guilt because he had been pursuing them. The officer, in a trance, walked in tight circles.

Thank goodness, one of the first drivers to come upon this disaster recognized the shock warning signs and immediately rendered first aid to the Patrolman. Other passing motorists checked on the six victims.

Ambulances and other officers were quick to respond to the scene. The Patrolman was the only one needing immediate medical attention but had gone into deep shock. He needed immediate doctor care, and the closest hospital, St. Agnes in Fresno, was 15 miles away.

One California Highway Patrolman on a motorcycle and another in a patrol car escorted the ambulance to the hospital in record time. The officer was now in competent hands.

Answers were needed. The Highway Patrolman could answer the last few minutes. What was the story behind this tragic happening?

It was 2:00 A.M. on the second Sunday of December. Three "*coyotes*" in the front seat of the cream-colored Cadillac picked up Ignacio, Ernesto, and Francisco at a prearranged place in the border city of Tijuana, Mexico. *{A coyote is a smuggler paid to sneak illegal aliens into the USA.}* The new rear-seat passengers had been promised safe passage through the U.S./Mexican border. Once on the American side, they would chauffeur them to the Fresno, California, area. They would be illegal immigrants within the hour, dead within twelve hours.

The *coyotes* knew when and which lane to take at the border. The officer staffing that lane was bribed. Therefore, the crossing was easy. The *coyotes* knew of two other checkpoints where they ran the danger of being caught with the three illegal young Mexicans.

However, they also knew how to avoid that from happening.

They successfully made it through the other two checkpoints.

A few hours later, they had breakfast in Los Angeles.

Shortly after noon, the Cadillac pulled into a driveway in Biola, California. (Biola is a tiny community of fewer than one thousand residents eight miles West of Fresno.)

The home the *coyotes* came to belonged to one of the illegal immigrant's close family members. The *coyotes* were to be paid here for smuggling the three young men.

Once they were paid, the *coyotes* would allow all three immigrants to exit the car simultaneously, which the poor illegals had not been allowed to do during the trip. Before this, only one illegal at a time had been allowed out of the car.

Unfortunately, the grownup residents of the home were in Fresno shopping. The few youngsters, who were home, were too young to provide detailed information. They just knew that their parents were in Fresno buying Christmas gifts. They could not say when their parents would be home.

They assumed, they told the *coyotes*, that the parents would be home before it got dark because that is what they had always done before. The youngsters had been instructed not to let anyone in or step out of the house. They were to watch movies by using the VCR.

The *coyotes* figured that the grownups would be home around 4:00 P.M. If the youngsters were correct, they faced at least a three-hour wait. Where to spend it?

Although this was the drop-off point, the *coyotes* would not allow the three young men out of the car without first being paid. *{Coyotes are armed and not shy about letting it known.}* Therefore, in a sense, they held the young men for ransom.

The coyotes decided that Fresno was too risky to kill time there. They feared a large city due to the more significant number of cops.

They chose to wait in Kerman; it would be safer there, or so they thought. In their way of thinking, "small-town cops are not as alert or as smart as large-city cops." In addition, they thought it would be much easier to keep an eye on the young men and detain them in a smaller town.

Kerman is a fast-growing town of about 15 thousand and is 8 miles southwest of Biola.

The *coyotes* intended to drive three miles from Shaw Avenue to Madera Avenue in a westerly direction. They would then turn south on Madera Avenue and travel five miles to Kerman. As the Cadillac entered Shaw, the driver did not notice a California Highway Patrolman approaching from the east since the vehicle was a reasonable distance away. (Shaw is a busy highway with a speed limit of 65.)

The Cadillac driver's entry onto Shaw was legal, but when he became aware of the Patrolman coming up behind them, the driver panicked and took off like a shot. Before the other two *coyotes* could calm him down, the Patrolman had turned on his flashing red lights. The chase was on!

Days later, the Patrolman recovered and related his story starting when he pulled in behind the Cadillac.

The officer said the Cadillac must have been going over one hundred miles per hour when it crashed at Shaw Avenue and Madera Avenue. He knew this because when his car's speedometer hit 90 mph, he backed off, and the Cadillac quickly pulled away. The Patrolman was calling ahead for help when the Cadillac rolled numerous times out of control.

The Patrolman figured the driver in the Cadillac saw the stop sign at the intersection of Shaw Avenue and Madera Avenue and the heavy cross-traffic and panicked and lost control of the car.

Such a foolish tragedy: forever silent three young men whose only crime was to make a better living for their families back in Mexico, and three dead law-breakers who came to an unfortunate ending.

CHANCE AGAINST NO CHANCE

It was May 1959, and the date of *'The Big Game'* was fast approaching.

The Big Game was the annual spring football game where the eighth-grade boys served as the opposing team for next-year's school team. Coach Kinney inaugurated this spring game when he became athletic director in 1953 when Cantua School opened its doors as a brand-new school in tiny Cantua Creek, California.

The best sixth and seventh graders for the next school year, and the seventh graders, who would be in the eighth grade in September, made up the school team.

According to Coach Kinney and his assistants, this future school team would be the best the school had ever fielded. He knew what he was talking about, for the nucleus of that group went on to win twenty-seven consecutive games over the next three years. In fact, in the first two years, no opponent even scored against them.

On the other hand, this year's eighth graders had been the worst group of athletes the school had ever suited up. Last fall, they hadn't even scored as the school's varsity football team, much less win a game. Basketball and baseball presented this group with the same results: they won one game in "*hoops*" and only two on the diamond.

As was customary, no coach or teacher was assigned to work with the eighth graders. They were on their own. They could practice or not; it was all up to them. Nobody would blame them; they were expected to lose anyway. They could easily give in to spring fever and not bother about practicing. Their girlfriends were waiting, and commencement was only weeks away.

Hurriedly, they called a team meeting for the eleven eighth-grade boys—eleven, no replacements!

Most of the boys had no desire to play. They did not wish to be "*dog meat*" for the future team.

Co-captain Larry Oaxaca realized they needed to be motivated, saying: "This is our chance to walk away winners. Never has an eighth-grade team beaten the future school team. Do you know why? Because they did not seriously or consistently practice. We will be the FIRST eighth-graders to win The Big Game!"

Defensive captain Ron Clark spoke next, "DEFENSE--the key to winning: DEFENSE!!! Coach Kinney has built his team for running plays, not passing, so we will use a 7-4 alignment. We will stop them one play at a time. We will put our best effort into the play in front of us. One play at a time will get us where we want to be at the end; WINNERS!"

The eighth-graders practiced as winners and were helped by their girlfriends, who rehearsed their cheers with the boys' workouts. Six girls had been the school's cheerleaders, so they had a strong squad.

On game day, the eighth-grade boys and girls were ready. It was the eighth grade versus the rest of the school.

The eighth-graders won the coin toss but chose to kick off as part of their master plan to show them (and, more importantly, themselves) the confidence they had.

Awesome! The eighth-graders held them to three plays and a punt! Larry and Ron repeatedly barked, "STOP THIS PLAY!!!"

The first quarter rolled by, then the second quarter. Still, the eighth graders gave little ground! Each play instilled more confidence in the underdogs. The future team would get a first down or two, but it was mostly a punt after three plays.

Consistent cheerleading by the girls kept the adrenaline of the boys pumping.

At the end of the third quarter, the eighth-graders overflowed with confidence while their opponents visibly lost theirs. Every time they forced another punt, it was like driving another nail into their coffin.

Larry called time out to remind the team, "...Yes, we are holding them from scoring, yet, we have to put some points on the board to win. We do NOT want to settle for a 0-0 tie! Yes, a tie would be a moral victory; but it is not a win. We want to win, DON'T WE? A win is within our grasp. Let us take it!" Ron chipped in by asking for better blocking for their running backs—Billy Ham and David Trent (the former was fast, the latter faster). They needed just a slight opening to go all the way.

 A few plays later, an eye-popping block by Ron cleared Billy for a significant gain on a misdirection play. The next play, a fake to Billy and pitchout to David, produced a 43-yard touchdown dash. Quarterback Ross Sánchez sneaked in for the point-after.

Now that they had scored, they focused on defense. Recall that the eleven boys played every single play of this big game. Though dog-tired, the eighth-graders immensely enjoyed stopping them play after play. Literal adrenaline kept them going. Before each play, Larry and Ron roared, "STOP THIS PLAY!!! STOP THIS PLAY!!!"

The future team made it easier on the "losers" by abandoning their game plan and taking considerable risks in their frantic effort to score. They tried passing but failed miserably since the team was built for ground attack.

As the final seconds ticked away, the eighth graders relished every second. The almighty future team dejectedly hung their heads. They kept their helmets on to hide their tears.

Coach Kinney and the fans could not believe what had transpired. They stared at the scoreboard in disbelief as if in a trance--HOME 0, VISITORS 7! WINNERS, AT LAST!

FLIPPED!

Gurdial, Sam, and I were in high spirits. My pals' parents had relented, allowing us to attend the basketball game between Sierra High School Chieftains and our high school, Tranquillity Union High Tigers. Hours later, our world would stop upside down, literally.

We three were best friends. I was a senior, while brothers Gurdial and Sam, natives of India, were sophomores. Perhaps due to their culture, their parents were particularly protective of them. It was rare for Gurdial and Sam's parents to consent to a night out for their sons. This game was to be the first game the brothers attended. It was also to be their last. The Chieftains and Tigers played on the last Friday of January 1963.

The three of us had put up excellent reasons in persuading Gurdial and Sam's parents of the importance of this game. This match promised a good game and the best chance for the

Tigers to defeat the Chieftains, which had not happened in my four years at Tranquillity High.

Sierra not only had been league champs the past three years, but they were undefeated the previous two. Although the Chieftains were not as talented this year as they had been the past three years, they were still at the top of the league standings.

The game was at the Tigers' old gym. For this reason, the Tigers had a slight advantage and might win. Sierra had crushed Tranquillity at Chieftain Gym 51-20 but rarely lost at home. In the league (North Sierra League), the gyms were on opposite ends of the spectrum. Tranquillity's gym was the oldest; Sierra's was the most modern.

The game started just as we had hoped. The Tigers refused to allow the taller Chieftains to run away with this game. At halftime, Tranquillity was down by only 5 points. Unfortunately, the Sierra Chieftains scored the first 12 points of the third quarter. The rout was on! The final score was 69-

39. The defeat kept intact the Tigers' losing streak against Sierra.

Downhearted, we headed home, twelve miles away. Still, we were more than thankful that there was no FOG--the main objection the parents of Gurdial and Sam used to convince them not to go to the game.

{In California's Central Valley, winter, "tule fog" is a significant problem causing numerous traffic accidents resulting in large pileups. The fog rises from the ground and settles in a layer, sometimes hugging the surface, causing ZERO visibility. When it is this bad, rather than shut down truckers, the California Highway Patrol acts as guide/scout to a caravan of cars traveling on Freeway 99.}

Neither of the brothers was willing to climb into the back seat. Each claimed it would be warmer in the front seat and the conversation would be more manageable.

That turned out to be a blessing. Our unyielding snugness protected us from serious injury just a few minutes later.

We had traveled only three miles when we suddenly encountered fog, **A WALL OF FOG!!!** The thick, white denseness reflected the high headlight beams at me, blinding me momentarily.

I panicked, thinking I was approaching the first curve's wicked 45-degree left turn. I turned too sharply and prematurely. Too late, I realized my mistake and over-corrected. At the same time, I was unaware that my right foot was pressing on the accelerator to brace myself. The car flipped over! How many times? We boys were at odds as to the number. The one certainty is that the Chevy ended up with wheels in the air on its top.

Thankfully, our being wedged as tight as sardines kept us from being ejected. As was typical of most cars that year, this 1952 vehicle was not equipped with seat belts.

The engine ran for a second or two when everything reached a standstill. I quickly turned off the engine. We were all asking at the same time about each other's condition. For a fact, we were incredibly fortunate, not a scratch on anyone!

When we managed to exit the upside car and walk to the road approximately 90 feet away, an uncle of one of the Tiger players stopped to help. The man reminded me to turn off the headlights which were still on. (*In my confused state, I had overlooked them.*)

While there, I pulled out the keys, which I had also forgotten. Thoroughly humiliated, we boys boarded the good Samaritan's vehicle. He drove us home.

My dad quickly recruited a friend to help him turn the Chevy right side up and get it home.

 Surprisingly, the car was not totaled. The only damage was to the car's roof, but the destruction was beyond repair.

On Saturday, the next day, my dad cut off the vehicle's top, thus turning the '52 Chevy into a permanent convertible. (Most likely, the only one of its kind!)

Gurdial and Sam's parents never allowed another night outing with me, and who can blame them?

 All in all, it had been a sorely disappointing night.

JOHN F. KENNEDY'S FIFTY-MILE-HIKE

CHALLENGE

The sixtieth anniversary of John F. Kennedy's fifty-mile hike challenge is in 2023. Few individuals took up that dare, and fewer completed that daunting task in less than twenty hours.

Let us recall one group's emotional experience in honor of all those champions of physical fitness who battled to complete the overwhelming feat.

President Kennedy *confirmed his commitment to improving the nation's fitness after his election in 1960 by publishing "The Soft American"* in ***Sports Illustrated***. Kennedy followed that by uncovering an executive order from President Theodore Roosevelt challenging U.S. Marine officers to finish fifty miles in twenty hours.

President Kennedy thought that to be a good gauge of a person's fitness and wondered out loud about the physical condition of his White House Staff. Press secretary Pierre Salinger deftly avoided that issue, whereas Attorney General Robert Kennedy, JFK's younger brother, embraced the test and covered the fifty miles through snow and slush!

However, the real brunt of the fifty-mile hike was with the public. Early in 1963, many Americans took the hike as a challenge from their President. High schools, especially, accepted JFK's invitation.

Nonetheless, many school administrations did not want the responsibility of fifty miles. Such school officials reasoned fifty miles was OK for mature Marines, but they chose a twenty-five-mile hike for their students. Still, President Kennedy acknowledged the students by putting his signature on a *"Certificate of Completion."*

Jack Delos Cook, head coach of Cross-Country and Track at Tranquillity Union High School in tiny Tranquillity, CA, refused to scale down President Kennedy's original request. Born in Golden City, MO, Cook emphatically stated, "One does not say NO to the President, and neither should one cut in half what he asks of us. Let it be known Tranquillity High School in Tranquillity, CA will not only tackle the fifty-mile-hike but will have the highest percentage of finishers in the Central California Valley, if not in the whole USA."

And, wouldn't you know it? He was correct: *'actions speak louder than words.'* Seventy-three percent of the 67 starters finished the hike. The minimum distance covered by those who *'failed'* was 31 miles, not bad for students who had never participated in any sport. Coach Cook, at age 45, completed the fifty miles. He was the only coach to accomplish this feat.

{Coach Jack Cook later coached at the University of Nevada, Reno, for over twenty years. His Wolf Pack won 16 conference titles. Cook's teams and athletes accomplished national rankings. Jack Delos Cook was selected to the WOLF Pack Hall of Fame—a rare and notable honor for a Nevada coach.}

Brother and sister Albert and Rosie Rios finished first in their genders. Both set national records. Albert's record—seven hours and 33 minutes--is safe for all eternity.

The current year is 2023, and one cannot help but wonder what John F. Kennedy would think of us now. If Americans were *'soft'* in the 1960s, what are we in this sedentary tech age?

OUT ON A LIMB

It was a hot summer day in 1975. Ross and his wife, Judy, visited with Judy's parents, Asa and Alene. Ross' in-laws lived in Cantua Creek, a tiny town in rural Fresno County, California.

All agreed; cooking dinner indoors on a gas stove was too hot. The heat from the stove would make it much more uncomfortable since Asa and Alene cooled their home with a swamp cooler.

Thus, Asa and Ross prepared for a barbeque in the backyard, where mulberry trees shaded the flat green Bermuda lawn. A light breeze combined with the shade made it bearable.

When the coals were ready, Judy brought a large plate of chicken to the grill. Judy stated that as her dad placed the chicken pieces on the grill, she could hear a kitten crying. Neither Asa nor Ross heard that and dismissed it. Judy retreated into the house.

Moments later, Judy returned with another plate full of hamburger patties. Again, Judy said she could hear a kitten. Once more, she was told she had heard things.

Judy stormed into the house with the cooked chicken pieces; she returned with her mother in tow.

Judy needed support, and she got it. Alene insisted, *"...no one move a muscle and listen."*

This time, a crying kitten was heard by all! But where? Four pairs of eyes went to the tree next to theirs when the kitty cried. Sure enough, they spotted the poor tabby kitty. The transfixed baby was trapped at the end of a limb. It was facing away from the tree's trunk and mortified at the thought of turning around to creep away from its dangerous position.

Judy, without delay, demanded her husband climb the tree and rescue the helpless, petrified kitty. He, at first, refused; but Judy was relentless, stating, "It is such a small baby and scared to death!"

Judy loved animals; Ross, not so much! Ross, against his will, consented, even though his father-in-law voiced not to bother with the poor animal. Asa added that it would figure its way off that limb, or its mama would rescue it.

Before Ross started his climb, he asked his wife to position herself directly beneath where the kitten was with her apron, ready to catch the stuck animal. Ross acknowledged he needed both hands to crawl back once he reached the kitten. He would not have a free hand to carry the kitten.

The closer Ross got to the terrified kitten, the louder and more constant it cried. As Ross was about to reach the kitten, everyone screamed, "HERE COMES THE MAMA, AND SHE IS MAD!!!"

In a flash, the large feline launched a furious attack on Ross' bare legs, the first things between her and her darling! Mama had no concern for herself; she was defending her baby!

Ross could not protect himself and keep his balance too. He came tumbling down! Fifteen feet later, he hit the ground!

Ross assessed his injuries. He could not tell which was worse: his legs lined with bloody scratches or his body in pain from the fall?

The failed hero jokingly asked his wife, "Why didn't you catch me?"

Judy's answer was, "I prepared for a kitten! I was not expecting you!"

O

Old as he was, he was ever on the alert for an opportunity to use his incredible marksmanship with his homemade slingshot. He recognized the world was in the Devil's hands, and one could find crime in every corner of the earth.

"He" was Orville, but few called him by his name. Orville was known only by "O" to those who knew him best. Some added a couple of syllables to his moniker: *"O the Sling*." Why? O always and everywhere packed a slingshot and ammo.

Often, *'self-righteous'* women viewed O as a *'bird killer'* if they saw his slingshot. Such women gave O a *'dirty'* look. Little did they know, O had given his solemn oath to his mother at age 11 never to shoot at a bird.

Orville merely shrugged off those *'dirty looks'* and hurried to conceal his *'weapon against wickedness'* from peering eyes.

At this instant, O had narrowly missed the starting point of a chance to exhibit his fantastic talent.

As O approached his vehicle in the Walmart parking lot with a cartload of groceries, he aimed his remote at his car. He witnessed an adult male about to seize a young lady from behind fifty feet beyond his vehicle. A black, newer SUV was within steps of the pair.

O could do nothing about those critical seconds he had missed. He had to work in the present. O accelerated his actions which consisted of: (1) retrieving his ammo, (2) placing it in the leather pouch, (3) aiming, and, finally, (4) releasing.

O achieved his payoff point in less time than it takes to spell Mississippi.

As O was doing his thing, the lady screamed more than once. Her first utterance was more like a surprised yelp. Her second was a cry for help, and the third was a concern for the safety of her baby.

{The police report listed it as an attempt to hijack her late-model SUV. The lady's baby was strapped in its car seat, so she loyally refused to surrender her car keys.}

The mother's frantic cries were so rapid; that few heard, and none rushed to the rescue of the terror-stricken woman. The few, mindful of what was happening, started filming with their smartphones—today's tech society!

Before the terrified mother finished her last shrieks, "MY BABY, MY BABY!!!" the hijacker repeatedly cried in agonizing pain, " MY EYE, MY EYE, MY EYE!!!

O's shot scored a bulls-eye, and the criminal's right eye socket was bleeding profusely! O's ammo—an old steel nut—was propelled by 10" natural latex bands, O's favorite.

 O did not expect, but was ready for, a second villain who entered the scene! This one was brandishing a gun and eyeing a target!

O did not hesitate; in what looked like one continuous motion, he went to his pocket, drew out another ¾-inch-steel nut, loaded, and released!

The speeding projectile moving at roughly 200 feet per second, struck the second hijacker in the temple, instantly causing him to lose consciousness. He took a nose dive! The horrified mother fled into her SUV and sped away!

O saw neither of these results, for he was laid low on the asphalt! His instant thought was he had slipped, and O quickly tried to rise. He could not! O was as weak as a baby! O felt a burning, excruciating pain in his left shoulder area and— BLOOD!!! He had been SHOT!!!

Two 'good Samaritan' men helped O up, while a third flipped a cart on its side for O to sit on. Once seated, another 'Samaritan,' a lady, applied a handkerchief to the wound and maintained pressure.

Instantly, police cars flooded the area. Amongst the police was the black SUV that had been the target of the would-be hijackers.

Police officers took control of the second hijacker, detained by a couple of husky men. O's temple shot recipient was still groggy and owned a horrendous headache.

Ambulances followed, none too soon, for O had begun to go into shock. Paramedics rushed to O's aid.

The second medics dashed to the criminal whose eye O had put out. The combination of pain and blood loss had caused him to pass out.

Medics tended to O to stabilize him before loading him into the ambulance. They dismissed the police's efforts to get a statement from him. They were wisely concerned, for O's pale skin, rapid breathing, and sweaty skin told them he was going into shock. Plus, the bullet wound only complicated matters, and, to make it even worse, O was 77 years old!

LA MIGRA! (IMMIGRATION!)

It was the first Saturday in June of 1973 and the third day of ranch work for Ross and Salvador. This hot day was the first time they had worked daylight hours.

Only three days before—Wednesday--Salvador had begged Ross to join him in working for a new landowner. At first, he protested but, in the end, agreed.

Ross was two days from finishing his school-teaching year at Cantua Elementary School. That meant he would have to conduct his fifth-grade class during the day and work through the nights of Thursday and Friday—60 hours without sleep!

This new owner had purchased a whole section of land, 640 square acres, from Giffen, Inc. He planned to grow wine grapes where only barley, cantaloupes, cotton, safflower, and tomatoes had grown before. Grapes were the first perennial crop tried on this section of land. This perennial crop would be the first in the 20,000 acres Giffen, Inc. farmed.

A labor crew planted baby vines of Bordeaux, Cabernet Sauvignon, Chardonnay, and Chenin Blanc on Thursday and Friday.

June temperatures approached 100 degrees; hence, Ross and Salvador had to water, at night, what was planted on that day, giving the newly-planted vines a fighting chance to survive the heat. Twelve-inch aluminum pipes, equipped with small sliding gates made of hard plastic, carried the irrigation water. The gates slid open to release water onto the eight-foot-wide space between the rows of new plants. Once the water reached the end of the field, these gates were closed, and another set opened. Depending on their distance from the well, ten to 12 sections could be opened simultaneously.

How had Salvador known about this new employer and a new job?

Earlier that week, Salvador shopped at Minnite's Market, Cantua Creek's only general goods store. Ralph Minnite told Salvador about the opportunity for a new job with a new landowner. If interested, could he recruit a co-worker?

Minnite said the manager of this property, Richard Bird, had asked him to find two respected, reliable laborers skilled in various ranch tasks. It was imperative the pair work well as a team.

Salvador and Ross lived on the northeast corner of this section which had just changed owners. Ross was Salvador's nearest neighbor. The pair's proximity to the worksite made it ideal. This new owner paid better than what Salvador was earning at Giffen, Inc., his current employer. This parcel had eleven dwellings, with a dirt road connecting them. The plot of land measured about three acres.

It made perfect sense for Ross and Salvador to accept this employment for these reasons.

Salvador was highly educated and graduated from reputable, higher-learning schools in Mexico. Ross enjoyed associating with Salvador. Since they were both well-educated, their conversations were intriguing and lively. As a bonus, Ross was learning proper Spanish from Salvador.

The two friends faced their first major hurdle this Saturday just before noon.

They were shoveling a hundred yards from each other. Suddenly, and in a panic, Salvador yelled to Ross, "LA MIGRA!!!" (This is a warning call announcing the appearance of immigration officers—INS, Immigration and Naturalization Service. INS was replaced by ICE, Immigration and Customs Enforcement in 2003.)

Salvador was NOT only illegally working in the United States but did NOT speak English, thus his alarm. Salvador and his wife, Irma, entered the country with a visitor's visa, but that '*green card*' stated they were NOT to work for wages in the USA. Result: Salvador and Irma were undocumented aliens!

Salvador and Irma had no intention of becoming permanent residents of the United States. Salvador's parents owned two successful businesses in San Miguel de Allende. San Miguel, an enchanting tourist attraction, won the "**Best City of the World**" award in 2017. Its location is in the state of Guanajuato.

The parents owned a general merchandise store and a bar side-by-side. The living residence was above the enterprises. This year marked the third summer Salvador had come here to earn money to upgrade the commercial establishments and construct housing for Irma and him.

This year, Irma joined her husband to accomplish the remodeling sooner. Salvador and his younger brother, Raul, would take over the business next calendar year.

Ross answered Salvador's warning call by instructing Salvador to stay calm and work toward him.

When they came together, they walked to the end of the field.

To avoid arousing suspicion, they walked to meet the INS officer who was walking in their direction, which unnerved Salvador. The second officer, his partner, drove the INS van to the opposite end of the dirt road to cut off Ross and Salvador if they ran.

The agent on foot was far enough away to give Ross plenty of time to settle Salvador down.

Ross instructed Salvador, "Stay calm and let me do the talking. If my hand goes toward my hat, repeat these words with confidence, '*It sure is*!'"

Salvador's pronunciation of the word '*sure*' worried Ross. It might be a dead giveaway!

The friends were rapidly approaching the officer!

Ross tried again. He asked Salvador to repeat the phrase, "*Yes, it is*!" This time Salvador nailed it. Ross told him to keep repeating it until they met the officer. Ross advised Salvador to look the officer directly in the face but keep an eye for when

Ross went to his hat. At that moment, Salvador should repeat the words he memorized.

Ross extended his hand to shake hands with the officer, saying, *"Good morning, officer!"* Salvador said nothing but did extend his hand. Salvador's eyes were intent on the officer's face.

Ross thought, *'so far, so good.'* Again, he addressed the officer, *"It sure is hot!"* while his hand went to his hat.

Salvador and the officer repeated like children in perfect harmony, *"Yes, it is!"*

The officer chuckled, turned, and walked away.

Years later, Ross was not surprised to learn Salvador had been elected state governor of Guanajuato!

DADDY, I DIDN'T LET GO! I DIDN'T LET GO!

You have undeniably heard of a father's beautiful love for his daughter. The common phrase used for that is *"Daddy's Girl."*

Not as prevalent, you might learn of a girl's love for her Daddy. An incident perfectly expresses a little girl's love for Daddy—a rare saying.

Though it was summer, it was not as blazing hot as is typical in California's San Joaquin Valley's central area—temperatures consistently exceed 100 degrees. The misadventure occurred on Tranquillity Elementary School's baseball grounds, where Ross was the eighth-grade teacher/coach.

With gusts exceeding forty miles, the potent wind of twenty to 25 miles felt more comfortable than the usual calm 100-degree day. Ross thought it ideal to take Ashley, who was not quite 4, for flying a kite the family had crafted the day before.

Ashley's mother, Judy, was not comfortable with that idea. She thought the wind was too strong for her little girl and was less sure of her husband's care for Ashley. Judy knew Ross had a propensity for poor choices, which greatly concerned her. (Ashley was Judy's firstborn, protecting her baby like a mama bear does her cub.) On this occasion, Judy was right again.

Ross carefully explained the steps of getting the kite into the air at the playground. (Ross had a lot to learn about children not eighth-grade age. Ross was a first-time father, and he learned an excruciating lesson on this day.)

Ross ran with the kite, holding on to the tail to put it into its flight, while Ashley held the spool of thick, cotton cord.

A forty-five-mile gust caught the kite and shot it into the atmosphere like a rocket. The spool unraveled too swiftly! Ashley could not control the spool, so she grabbed the cord with her tender hands as the extreme wind threatened to rip it from her delicate hands. The cord's upward, speedy movement through Ashley's hands cut into her palms.

Too late, Ross saw the danger a hundred feet from him! Desperate, Ross yelled at Ashley to let go of the cord; he kept repeating his cry as he ran full speed to Ashley's rescue.

Despite the burning pain and the blood, Ashley refused to *"...disappoint Daddy"* by relinquishing her grip. Her love for her Daddy was more robust than the burning pain and blood which ran through her clutched, tiny hands.

Despite his actions, Ross did not save his little girl from the burning cord. He swooped her in his arms and rushed her to the safety of her mother's arms, foolishly hoping Judy could undo what he had stupidly caused.

Ross kept telling Ashley how sorry he was for hurting her. They drove the four blocks home in an instant! Still, the pain did not keep Ashley from wrapping her arms tightly around her Daddy's neck and, with her face pressed against his, declared, "DADDY, I DID NOT LET GO! I DIDN'T

LET GO!!! I DIDN'T LET GO!!!"

"VANISHED" SOCK

Have you heard of the *"vanished sock"?* Quite likely, you have. Unless you are new to earth, you have experienced it. But it was not always so.

In the beginning, missing socks had an accounting. The women washed at the river; they smacked the clothes on rocks to loosen the filth. Yes, they did, on occasion, lose a sock. But they knew exactly where it had gone; the current had carried it away.

Meanwhile, the sun and wind served as dryers. The modern dryer was not even a dream yet.

Time passed; the washboard was invented, and clothes were reprieved from being swatted against rocks. Naughty boys and bad dogs were responsible for the few socks which did not make it safely to the drawers.

The sun and wind were still stuck with the task of drying. Nonetheless, ingenious minds set out to invent an alternative way of drying clothes.

Next, the wringer washer made her entrance. What a mean machine that was!!! It delighted in flattening fingers, hands, and arms! Other than to wash them, it paid no mind to socks, not yet! This horrid machine's appetite was only satisfied by human flesh.

Despite the growing population overtaxing them, there was nothing to help the sun and wind.

Somewhat late, man admitted his mistake in developing the wicked wringer washer when women began blasting this arm-consuming beast with their husbands' shotguns! He set out to improve the washer. This thinking resulted in the present-day machine.

Finally, and much to the joy of the sun and wind, a genius came out with the dryer. Yet, this helpful invention brought about a different peccadillo.

Thus was the onset of the *"vanished sock."* Odd, it never occurs in pairs. Did the washing machine find its perfect partner-in-crime in the dryer? Or, since they cohabit, did the duo put their heads together and come up with this idea of taking our socks one at a time so that we would not suspect them? We will never know; they are not talking. Does this sound familiar?

Just recently, I was victimized. One of my favorite socks went missing. Try as I might, recovery was in vain. I had to confess; another sock had become a casualty of the devilish behavior of the washer/dryer dual.

Where do the chosen (*vanished*) socks go? Is there sock heaven? Do you suppose that instead of the streets of Heaven being lined with gold, they are paved with a collage of *"vanished"* socks?

The day of my vanished sock is marked—I joined the millions who have become prey to the mischievous machines. You will soon join us if you have not already!

OVER THE FENCE!

Ross needed to return to his classroom to prepare for a particular lesson the following school day. The family had just finished supper when Valery asked if she might accompany her daddy.

Surprisingly, Valery's mom, Judy, allowed her to go on this outing with her dad since they would be gone for less than two hours.

Val had just turned three and saw herself as very independent. She could be of help to her father.

Tranquillity, where Ross taught/coached, is fifteen miles from Kerman, where the family lived.

Since it was winter and already dark, Ross locked the door once they were inside. Work went quickly and smoothly, and Valery was of assistance--perhaps, too helpful.

When Valery required a bathroom break, Ross walked her out of the classroom and toward the bathroom. All at once, Valery turned around and dashed to close the door. Since her daddy had explained the necessity of a locked, closed door, it was natural for Valery to do what she did.

Unfortunately, Ross had left his keys on top of his desk! His pickup key, the house key, the gate key, and the classroom key were all together. They were sunk!

Ross could not "*break*" into his classroom no matter what he tried. Ross and Val were locked out of the classroom, but they were also trapped inside the school grounds, for without the gate key, they could not go to the school janitor's home to get help.

The janitor respected and admired Ross, for he kept a clean and orderly classroom, making her work quicker. Her home and the school were on the same street.

As much as Ross hated it, he and Val would have to scale the six-foot chain-link fence. It would not pose a problem for

Ross, but Val was only three and could not be expected to climb, go over the fence, and descend.

The only way Val could go over the fence and back down on the opposite side was for Val to hang on tight to her dad's neck as he did the scaling.

Valery refused. She was not afraid for herself but feared choking her daddy. Val was more mature than her age and recognized the danger.

Finally, Ross convinced Val that he could hold his breath long enough to climb the fence, ascending and descending. Ross squatted down so Val could wrap her arms around her daddy's neck and her legs around his tummy.

Despite her age, Val kept calm and did a fantastic job holding on to her dad as they climbed and descended the six-foot chain-link fence.

Once on the ground outside the school grounds, the six-block walk to the janitor's home was *"...a piece of cake."*

EARRINGS

He, all alone, waited at the counter while the associate replaced the battery in his watch.

A middle-aged lady approached the earring section of the jewelry store right next to him. Her eyes twinkled as they surveyed the resplendent earrings.

The man immediately recalled that glistening of the eyes. He had seen it before. His dear-departed wife had the same glow in her eyes when eyeing earrings.

He battled tears and stated, "Nothing like new earrings!"

The lady blushed and responded, "A woman's weakness!"

The man replied, "You need not be embarrassed. My wife, before she passed, had the same look on her face when viewing earrings.

"She had dozens of them. No, I dare say she had a hundred or thereabouts. Yet, whenever she lost one earring, she went into desperation mode. We had to turn the house inside out, looking for that missing earring. And, if we found it, what a glorious feeling for her and me. She would wear that pair for days after, careful where she set them down. Of course, I made it a point to say something positive about how that pair complimented her looks.

"But I remember best when she came upon a new pair she coveted. Her eyes had that look about them that, even now, I recall well. She would position them next to her ears, look in the mirror, and say, 'Aren't they gorgeous? How do they look on me?'

"My recurrent answer was, 'You're only holding them next to your ears! I cannot tell. Put them on!'"

"Her habitual comeback, 'No, they are too expensive! I do not need them. Let's go!'"

"She would gently, lovingly put them down, turn softly, and slowly start to walk away,

"I invariably recognized my cue and would implore, 'Are you sure about this? At least try them on! Maybe they will not look the same when you are wearing them. This way, there will not be any regrets.'"

"Her answer, which I knew by heart, 'Well, if you insist, I will put them on, just to make you happy!'"

"Once the earrings were fitted to her ears, I remember only too painfully the words she would implore, 'If you get them for me, I will never ask for anything else!'"

The man struggled to get the last statement out as tears flowed freely!

He fought to compose himself and almost whispered, "What I would give to hear her voice those words again."

PS: This incident occurred in the Super Walmart across from the Walmart headquarters in Bentonville, AR.

FREE ALL DOGS!

When Judy turned her Ford van into the family's driveway, Ross, her husband, could see something was wrong.

At the end of the driveway and just in front of the garage was Ross and Judy's older daughter, Ashley, crying! Her husband, Josh, was consoling her.

Ashley's younger sister Valery hurriedly jumped out of the vehicle before it stopped. She rushed to her sister's side, asking what was wrong.

Ashley was too pained to speak. Each time she commenced talking, she would break out sobbing.

Josh said, "All our dogs are missing, and we are pretty sure the city workers took them. "Our neighbors say they witnessed as uniformed city-of-Kerman workers opened our side gate and entered our backyard. Less than a minute later, they saw *Hank* bolt through our now-opened gate and run toward your home." {*Hank knew the way since Ashley walked him there often.*}

Josh breathed and continued, "Three city workers then exited the backyard. Two of them were carrying *Sela* and *Nolan, respectively*. The third person carried a long pole with a net at its end. They put *Sela* and *Nolan* in the animal-control van and took off toward your house, presumably after *Hank*.

We looked around your house, but no Hank, Sela, or *Nolan*. We called City Hall, but we only got a recording stating their office hours because of the late hour, and we have no idea where the dog pound is."

Josh, again, paused to comfort Ashley. He resumed, "Our neighbors say that the city workers arrived at our home at about 4:00 PM. We got home from work around 5:30 and have been looking ever since.

"We expected you home about ten because you called right after your plane landed to let us know." (*Ross, Judy, and Valery had just returned from a trip to Northwest Arkansas.*)

Ross was furious! In September, he had had a run-in with Kerman City Hall over Tosca, his guard dog. It was now the middle of November. The issue? Ross did not confine his 75-pound German shepherd because it would not allow her to protect BOTH Ross's pickup and gardening trailer while he worked in the backyards of his clients.

Ross sued the city in Small Claims Court for criminal negligence because one of the city workers, not the animal-control officer, had shot *Tosca* with a tranquilizer gun without cause.

{*Property crime is ridiculously high in California and even worse in Kerman due to the unethical behavior of all city officials, from cops to city maintenance workers.*}

Valery immediately rushed Tosca to her vet in Fresno—20 miles away.

In the meantime, Ross was at City Hall raising Cain about the tranquilizer and size of dosage—information needed to give the proper antidote.

According to Tosca's veterinarian, Tosca came ever so close to cardiac arrest due to the carelessness of the city workers using a dosage three times greater than necessary to tranquilize Tosca. The ignorant maintenance worker did not know how to assess the proper dosage for Tosca's weight. The city worker talked the animal-control officer into allowing him to shoot Tosca with the tranquilizer gun.

{Two years after Ross's family moved to Arkansas, the city workers were convicted of running a theft ring using their position as cover.}

Ross first informed Josh and Ashley he knew the location of the dog pound, then promised to recover their dogs before midnight.

Josh hurried to get his car to transport the dogs. Josh and Ashley's home was less than two blocks from Ross and Judy's.

Ross entered his garage/workshop. Here, he kept all the tools he used to work on his landscaping maintenance equipment. Ross exited armed with a hacksaw, a hammer, a crowbar, and work gloves.

Josh returned at about the same time. With rescue firmly set in Ross' mind, they took off toward the dog pound. Operation "*Free All Dogs*" was underway!

Once they got to the dog pound, Josh expressed fearful concern about the legality of what they were about to do.

Ross responded, "What do you call what the city workers did to your pets? STAY IN THE CAR IF YOU WANT! I AM FREEING THE DOGS!"

Josh required more persuasion. He asked, "How do we know if our dogs are even in there?" (*There was a chain-link fence surrounding the whole area, and the kennels were a reasonable distance from this fence. The height of the fence was 8 feet.*)

Ross told Josh to step out of the car and call his dogs. They had parked right in front of two large, drive-through, swinging, chain-link gates, which came together in the center of the driveway.

There was just enough moonlight to see the thick chain wrapped around the posts of the gates with a heavy-duty lock to keep people from using regular-sized bolt cutters on either the chain or the lock.

Ross prepared for these barriers and brought a heavy-duty hacksaw with a new steel-cutting blade.

Josh stepped out of the car and practically whispered the dogs' names. Ross barked out, "LOUDER!!! Remember, the city workers went into your backyard to get them illegally. You have witnesses. They broke into your private property! We are recovering your illegally taken dogs."

Ross could feel the adrenaline running through his veins. Ross probably would have welcomed a confrontation with those idiots in his state!

Now, much louder, Josh called his dogs. They responded excitedly, happy barking, but so did all the other dogs. However, they must have been in pens, or they would have dashed to the gate.

Ross started working his hacksaw. In less than a minute, he cut the chain in two. They hurried to find the pens about 60 yards beyond the gate.

Ross easily cut, lock after lock, releasing Josh's pets and other dogs.

Again, Josh was hesitant about freeing other people's dogs. Ross pointed out it had to be this way. If they broke free only Josh's dogs, the city workers would immediately know who did it. Besides, he pointed out that these other dogs most likely were abducted the same way as his animals.

{The city workers were not content with stealing household/gardening items; they abducted dogs, too. They sold them to a 'black market' for medical trials when they had a good load.}

Ross and Josh loaded Ashley's three dogs and two smaller other dogs with incredible difficulty. They left the remaining dogs to go where they pleased. Hopefully, they would find their way home.

The small car jammed full of dogs, the heroes drove back to the city and released the dogs that were not theirs at the city park.

Triumphantly, they went home. The time was just before midnight—the hour Ross had promised to rescue Ashley's pets.

{No one from city hall, the dog catcher, or city workers confronted Ross about this incident.

A REWARDING HAIRCUT

My friend Jack is a retired policeman. His career spanned from the mid-thirties through the mid-sixties, when "*Protect and Serve*" meant just that, and an officer of the law was respected and admired. Jack has always enjoyed life, and perhaps due to his law-enforcement experience, he is quick to notice things, even at his age.

Lately, Jack's health began a plummeting trend. He was rightly depressed to learn he had liver cancer. At first, Jack vigorously rejected any treatment. Finally, his family prevailed in giving him a fighting chance and accepted his chemo and radiation regimen.

This medical treatment took a heavy toll on Jack. He lost over 50 pounds! Such an existing condition caused problems, and going without a haircut for months gave him a haggard look. He lost all will—refused everything, including eating.

Mary Lou, his wife, despaired at his condition.

I chauffeured Jack to his barbershop before he was diagnosed with cancer. Jack enjoyed those times immensely. He loved the company and delighted in having a listening ear to his many police stories. Believe me, as a lifelong police officer in Los Angeles. Jack had experienced plenty. After his haircut, Jack would treat me to lunch. We had memorable times.

That all came to an end when Jack got knowledge of his cancer! While taking treatments for a few months, Jack refused to eat or agree to a haircut. Mary Lou was distraught, for she correctly sensed Jack had lost his will to live. Her beloved Jack was wasting away.

Mary Lou was very much troubled. She attempted something that might help her dear Jack.

Mary Lou did not want to impose on me because I had married while Jack was receiving cancer treatments. Instead, she phoned me and asked for directions to the barbershop I used to drive him to so their married daughter might drive Jack to get a haircut.

She hoped an outing for something other than Chemo/radiation treatment might lift his spirits.

I immediately offered to drive Jack to the barbershop myself. Mary Lou turned down my move apologetically, stating Jack would not accept. (Jack recoiled at the thought of someone besides family seeing his condition.) So, as I was giving Mary Lou directions on how to get to the barbershop, my wife, Betty, volunteered to cut Jack's hair. (Betty cut not only my hair but our neighbors' as well. She took great pride in her impeccable talent.)

Jack declined Betty's proposal—the shame of his condition once again.

The pause allowed me time to think of a way to convince Jack to have me drive him to the barbershop. I requested Mary Lou tell Jack I missed his company and would love to see him. My words did the trick! I arranged to drive Jack to the barbershop the following morning.

I was surprised as I arrived at Jack's home to pick him up! Jack had reconsidered! He would let Betty cut his hair!

I was overjoyed. I called Betty to let her know we were coming, giving her time to set up her equipment.

Jack got a much-needed hair trimming after introductions. WHAT A TRANSFORMATION!

Betty and I received a wonderful phone call from Mary Lou the following day. Almost in tears, she let us know Jack greatly admired his haircut. He exclaimed it was the best haircut he had ever had. After getting home from *'the barber,'* Jack headed straight for the shower. But he stopped long enough to ask Mary Lou to fix something to eat—he was hungry!

Now openly crying, Mary Lou stated Jack was eating a hearty breakfast at that moment—a second meal in less than twenty-four hours! Before his haircut, the family had to plead for Jack to eat a mouthful now and then.

Well, by this time, Betty and I were also crying. That was some haircut—life-changing!

ME vs. ANTS

Did I tell you about my battle with ants? No, I suppose I did not. Maybe my conscience blocked my bravado. I do not know. Anyway, here is the story of my conflict with the ants.

Shortly after moving into my newly-purchased home in Bella Vista, Arkansas, I noticed tiny critters here and there. Quickly I pinched myself twice because, after the first pinch, the wee unwelcomed guests were still visible.

For the time being, I avoided the matter. I was sure the ants would be gone by morning. Sleep did not come easy. Did I see things? If so, are they friendly? Were the ants, perhaps, bringing a housewarming gift? Well, you can imagine my dreams that night.

Well, morning came, and so did the teeny invaders. What to do? What to do?

Determined only by my imagination or lack of coffee, I began reading the *Democrat-Gazette* while drinking my morning brew.

I avoided looking at the area where I had seen the quick-marching pests with all my being. Yet, I couldn't focus on what I was reading! I found myself having to read the same paragraph over and over.

"THAT'S IT!!!" I pronounced loudly to no one since I live alone. I hurried to my office and retrieved a magnifying glass. That was my first step in my battle with the ants—identify the enemy!

Sure enough, there they were! They numbered in the dozens, perhaps hundreds, marching as if going to war—beautiful lines, with equal spacing between each teeny-weeny warrior. The itsy-bitsy soldiers were attacking me! How dare they? Don't they realize how minuscule they are?

If it is war they want, it's war they will get! My buddy James had confrontations with ants before, and I recall he used baby powder as his primary weapon. (I did not know why James employed baby powder to defeat the ants, but I soon found out.)

I showed no mercy—remember, the ants started it—I poured powder all over them, their trail, and their entrance into my kitchen. If a bit of powder is good, a lot is better.

I waited.

Not having much patience and doubting the power of the powder, I decided on a trip to the library to research strategic military maneuvers in my *"Battle with the Ants."*

A small platoon of ants was waiting for me on my return. They were all dressed in their best military white, or was that the baby powder? What was it they were thinking? Were they communicating with me?

The leader saluted, or was he trying to shake off the baby powder? He spoke firmly and with great authority.

You do not have to believe me; you weren't there. The leader stated they (the army of ants) were not consulted about the change of food providers in their home—I thought it was my home! He added, what is more, they were not about to move. They liked it here. Next, and even louder, he declared they allowed the previous humans residency in exchange for food. The giant beings left sustenance on the table and even made sure some nourishment made it to the older, weaker ants by letting it drop to the floor.

{It never occurred to me, until after the ordeal, that I could understand the ants and, more surprisingly, hear them! You see, I am hard of hearing. This incident made me believe I have trouble hearing people because I have ant DNA. My dear-departed mother and ex-wife always claimed I was much more than a little weird. I had two previous battles with fire ants, both of which I lost. That may explain why I speak their lingo.}

As you might imagine, I was not in agreement with their remarks. I was just as firm, if not louder, as I stated, "Things have changed. I am the OWNER of this home and will not share it with ants. Do you realize it is unsanitary for us to share quarters? I am as concerned for me as I am for you; I might give you the flu or a serious cold! Your head might fly off with a hard sneeze! I empathize with you, but I can take my leftovers to a designated area where you can easily and more comfortably access them. I will also see to it that you always have water available."

Finished, I was nervous because, as a six-year-old, I tried to give the *"evil eye"* to a hill of fire ants and had barely come out alive. Did these ants know this? Could they read my thoughts?

The ants huddled for less than a minute and returned with their answer. They agreed I was to provide food and water for them so long as they did not enter their house—they still refused me ownership! I was not to ever use any weapons on them, especially that white powder. They declared that baby powder was like broken glass pieces to me! And they have SIX legs! *{So, there it was! My friend James is not as dumb as I thought!}*

Treaty is not necessary. The ants' word is their bond. PEACE!

GABRIEL

Ross had just purchased a home in Bella Vista, Arkansas. The previous owner left a few space-taking objects, including a complete roof for a shed. Though the roof measured just eight by 7 feet, it made no sense. That is all there was, and it was sitting on the ground. Its location was odd--the very back of the backyard.

Ross wanted the roof out of his yard since it was unsightly. He advertised it and other articles on a radio program that allowed listeners to sell, buy, or give away items.

Finally, on Ross's fourth try at calling for someone to come and take the roof and the six other helpful material things, Eddie and his nine-year-old son, Gabriel, came to retrieve the large pieces.

The trio easily and quickly loaded the other articles— hydroponic trays three feet square into Eddie's Honda van.

The fact that they were a uniform size made it easy. They locked into each other like egg cartons.

The roof posed a different, complicated problem, too large to load as a unit. But, due to the clever positioning of the articles already placed inside the van, there was still room.

Eddie glanced at the setting sun and addressed Gabriel, "Son, what do you think? Can we dismantle the roof and take it on this load? Are you game?" *(Eddie and Gabriel had come from Gravette, 20-25 minutes away.)*

Little Gabriel crossed his arms, as undoubtedly, he had seen his dad and grandpa (as it turned out) do. Gabriel stated, "We don't have the tools, Dad!"

To this, Ross quickly replied, "I have a cordless Ryobi drill and the correct heads (*the heads of the screws were star-shaped*). I am confident we have enough daylight left to finish the job."

Ross brought out his Ryobi tool, and as he handed it to Eddie, Gabriel intercepted it. Puzzled, Ross looked at Eddie.

Eddie pronounced, "This is his element. He loves tools, and his grandpa has taught him how to use most of them. He takes special pleasure in handling the tools. Do you mind if Gabriel works your power drill?"

"If you say Gabriel can handle the Ryobi, let's have Gabriel take it apart while we haul the boards to the van and load them," Ross declared. *(The vehicle was parked 150 ft away, but it was all uphill at a 45° angle.)*

Eddie carefully supervised Gabriel at the beginning of unscrewing the three-inch screws. Although Gabriel did not have the skill of an older person, he managed just fine. Additionally, the boy was not near as fast as an adult would have been, but Eddie patiently encouraged his son.

Being a retired schoolteacher, Ross loved what he was seeing. A dad worked with his son patiently, thoughtfully, and, most importantly, with much love. Ross delighted in

NOT hearing criticism, threats or put-downs, common child-abuse signs. Instead, he witnessed a loving father give support and guidance and do so with the utmost patience.

One could see Gabriel was the recipient of such loving care from birth. The confidence, dedication, and respect he was applying to his work showed. Though the number of screws to be removed was huge, Gabriel did not complain or threaten to quit, and the youth asked for help only when the screws were at a wicked, difficult angle. This lucky child would **NOT** be one of the 6 million abused children who require counseling as adults.

At that moment, Ross dearly wished he had a video camera or a *'smart phone'* capable of recording action like the antique home-movie camera. That brought up the thought, *'Gabriel probably knows how to operate such a phone, thanks to Eddie, a perfect example of what a father should be.'*

Progress was slower than it would have been with an adult manning the drill, but no one minded. Eddie and Gabriel benefited not only by acquiring a roof but also by working together.

Ross, for his part, was enjoying such a tender, loving time between father and son. He paused to wipe away the silent tears, pretending it was sweat, for this experience brought back the few yet precious memories Ross had enjoyed with his long-dead father.

They finished the work just before dark. The Honda van accommodated the entire load. Gabriel fondly returned the power tool to Ross and said, "Thank you very much for allowing me to use such a nice tool."

Ross replied, "Gabriel, it was my pleasure to see you work it and enjoy yourself. You have a great dad, who loves you, and it shows. I hope you are aware of just how blessed you are. He handed Gabriel a bag of hot buttered popcorn to munch during the ride home.

DEATH of a DEAR FRIEND

A very dear friend passed away recently! It is easy to say the person lived an exemplary life at his funeral. In this case, it is no different, except that GERALD WAYNE REEVES lived that praiseworthy life.

One would have to go back to Bible times to find persons who, perhaps, were like Gerald. But even those characters had significant flaws; the Bible points out. In Gerald's case, you would be hard-pressed to find *one person* with some gripe against him.

Gerald Wayne Reeves liked every person he met. He treated each human being with kindness and respect. His honesty was well-recognized by his community. He never lied to anyone, so he had no reason to think anyone would lie to him. Perhaps, Gerald saw the world through rose-colored glasses, which served him well if he did. And, no, Gerald

Wayne Reeves was not "touched," not naïve, and not slow. Quite the opposite is true.

Gerald was lovingly teased by his older brothers as the youngest of four boys. They had him believing he was adopted for a while and that his real name was '*Virgil.*' And how did Gerald take it? He saw it as a sign of how special he was to his brothers. As an adult, Gerald heard it as an esteemed nickname whenever one of his brothers called him 'Virgil,' a term of endearment shared only between brothers.

Every one of Gerald's brothers was athletic and excelled in sports. Gerald preferred horse riding and spent much time improving his reading while reading the Bible. He became an expert at both.

Before turning forty, Gerald Wayne Reeves was an elder in his congregation, no surprise being a trustworthy, compassionate, loving man. Brother Reeves was everyone's choice to hear and endeavor to solve his concern. Despite being a husband and father of two, Gerald always had time for those counseling calls.

Why are there people like Gerald? And how come the number of people like Gerald is so minute?

In Gerald's very early life, one incident declared what kind of person he would be for the rest of his life.

Gerald was six at the time this happened. Give extreme attention to what the young lad loyally REFUSES to reveal.

Gerald came to the nurse's office, cradling his left arm with his right arm. The school nurse could immediately tell the arm was broken. She asked Gerald his name and how he happened to break his arm. (Simultaneously, she fitted Gerald with an arm sling.)

Gerald's face was the same color as his broken arm, almost red, giving his soft-blond hair a cotton look. He said, "My name is Gerald Wayne Reeves, and I was trying to fly but did not swing high enough to take off!"

The puzzled nurse queried, "Gerry, what made you think you could fly?"

"My name is Gerald Wayne Reeves," Gerald emphatically exclaimed.

Again, the nurse asked, "No one calls you Gerry or Cotton? Please explain why you were trying to fly."

"My name is Gerald Wayne Reeves, not Gerry or Cotton. Everyone calls me Gerald Wayne Reeves. I did not wait till I was swinging way up high. I jumped off the swing too soon, so I did not fly."

"Gerald Wayne Reeves, who put you up to this? Who told you you could fly if you got high enough on the swing and jumped off?" Asked the nurse, still working on his broken arm.

"It is my fault. The boys told me if I got on the swing, they would push me and push me and push me until I got high enough so I could jump and start flying. I was not high enough to fly. That is all!" Gerald finished gritting his teeth in pain and would say no more.

{Before you brand the boy dimwitted, consider two things: 1) the lad is six years old, and 2) most boys his age can fly in their dreams.}

The nurse just shook her head. She adjusted the soft sling for Gerald Wayne Reeves' broken arm. An ice pack had been placed underneath his comfortably-wrapped arm and another on top of the arm. She picked up the phone to call his home.

You often hear, "When they made him, they broke the mold!"

Whoever first coined this phrase must have been thinking of GERALD WAYNE REEVES!

MY CARDINALS

My vehicle is equipped with privacy glass all around. The tint is such it rules out visibility to the inside of the SUV, and the darkness gives the glass a mirror effect. This reflection plays a significant role in my cardinals' story.

You may know cardinals are territorial. They claim areas as small as two acres or as large as ten acres. Once the couple, who mate for life, establish their domain, they remain there until death.

The male cardinal—enrobed in its beautiful crimson color—defends its territory with loud yet melodious whistles while perched atop the tallest vantage point in its dominion. Such a warning is usually enough. If a fight ensues, the female will assist by taking on the female claim jumper.

The fun, sunny days came with the end of the long, hard winter we had in the northwest area of Arkansas. With their warmth, the clean, clear days brought instant greenery to vegetation. My cardinals stood out with their glorious colors against the verdant trees and bushes.

Unfortunately, sunny days also brought an invader couple into my cardinals' kingdom! *"What to do? What to do?'* That question was the immediate thought of my cardinals. My male cardinal started his warning with his distinctive, musical whistling—*GET OUT AND STAY AWAY!*

Next, my male macho bird flittered to see if the infiltrator fowl was still near my vehicle. YES! THE VIOLATOR WAS THERE!

My feathered friends glided to perch on the driver's window sill and confronted the lazy pair who dared attempt to steal their home instead of working to find their own.

The male approached male, and female faced female! Still, the intrusive couple only mimicked my cardinal pair*! The shame of it all--coming into our home and mocking us!*

On cue, my cardinals tore into the jokers! Their blows were futile! My crushed couple retreated to gather their thoughts and regroup. Beaks bruised and dignity damaged, they had to admit they had not hurt the enemy. *"These aggressors seem to have shields that protect them,"* my cardinals concluded.

My cardinal's male ego was offended, and he wanted satisfaction. Fearful for his wife, he asked her to remain behind. This battle was like no other he had fought before.

Again! Same results! The male fluttered back to his partner. She asked, *"Did you drive him away? Did you hurt him badly? Was the female there?"*

My male cardinal answered, *"Slow down! Too many questions! I have a horrendous headache from pecking their shield. And, no, the female must have been hiding, just like I told you. These foes know our tricks as if they know what we are thinking."*

My female cardinal soothingly and softly told her hubby, "*You tried, Honey, and got only a headache. Perhaps we should let them have our home, Dear.*"

My male cardinal shot back, "*NEVER! Here is what we are going to do. From now on, we will drop our deposits on their shield. The foul, offensive odor of our privy will drive them away.*"

"*You are my man!*" shouted the female. "*I knew you would come up with a solution. Let us start depositing right now!*"

A cloth cover for my vehicle will be delivered tomorrow.

ACROSS THE FENCE

The elderly, small male moved into a duplex without much fanfare. It had not been by choice but by necessity he had relocated here.

For years, the man, Edwin, had lived in senior housing. And before the *'have-no-choice'* move to the duplex, that is where he called home. Nearing the end of his first year of residency in senior apartments, Ed had to be recertified for his second-year lease.

Edwin had started helping his neighbors to avoid boredom and for exercise. Not thinking ahead, he had started cleaning the front patios of seniors unable to handle the task. Ed swept off spider webs, scraped off mud dubber nests, cleaned the windows, and finished by blowing clean the entire area.

Edwin saw the need and first asked seniors if he could help them by doing the clean-up job.

Word got around, and Edwin was as busy as he wanted. Yet, most seniors insisted on paying him. This income bumped Ed over the break-off limit, and Edwin no longer qualified to live in the senior apartments.

Edwin's new duplex cost him almost $400 a month more than he paid for senior housing, creating an unyielding predicament for the seventy-eight-year-old man. Ed suffered from clinical depression and was panic-stricken; his financial situation might cause him to fall into a *"black-hole"* episode. (*Such episodes resulted in excruciating mental anguish; it took months of new medication and counseling before relief finally came.*)

No matter how Edwin adjusted his budget, the results were the same—a drastic cutback was required! He knew he would make it if he only survived the first month.

On the first morning at his new home, Ed debated: should he have two pieces of toast or just one with his coffee? He settled on two rather than just one figuring the empty slot would cost him money regardless.

After finishing the first piece of toast, Edwin poured a second cup of coffee and stepped out on the back porch to enjoy the quiet scene and sunny morning.

The couple next door owned a dog; the animal immediately came to the cyclone fence and barked once. The hound/terrier mix dog viewed the new resident with rapt attention!

Ed greeting the middle-sized male dog walked over to the fence and continued, "What a good boy you are! Most dogs would bark nonstop, but you are a nice doggie choosing to learn by carefully observing your new neighbor. You need to be rewarded! Stay right here!"

Edwin returned with the second piece of toast for his new friend. Ed quickly broke it into portions that fit through the cyclone fence's grid and fed the friendly dog. The ready and willing canine made short work of the toast and, with happy yelps, pleaded for more.

Edwin explained that was all there was, told him his name, and asked the nice-looking dog his name. Of course, the friendly pooch had no answer other than wagging his tail ecstatically.

Thus began a friendship that significantly transformed Edwin's negative feelings. Once again, man's best friend had come to the rescue. The new duplex tenant had something to look forward to every morning. Edwin would not be visiting the *"black hole"* anytime soon!

EDUCATED BY SUNI

Recently, I house-sat for my daughter, Ashley. She and her husband, Josh, have a collection of animals requiring someone to be on location to look after them while they are away.

The six miniature horses were no problem. The three cats, likewise, posed no issues. (*In case you did not know, cats are incredibly independent, so much so cats have the attitude they own us instead of vice versa.*)

Now, the dogs were a different story!

My daughter recognized that, so she arranged to have Suni kennel-boarded. Suni is their newest dog. I vigorously objected! My daughter and son-in-law presumed Suni to be too spirited for a 78-year-old small man.

Suni is a Labradoodle nearing her first birthday. Yet, this chocolate-colored, curly-haired canine, said to be unable to reason, feel, or sense would shame some people. Though seventy pounds, she believes she is a lap dog and owns more bad habits than good ones.

Suni had lived her first few months in a no-kill shelter. Now and again, she would be adopted by a prospective new owner, only to be returned—four failed homes! To them, Suni was too lively. (*Sad, but true, this is a much-too-common problem—pet owners unwilling to invest the time to train their new pet!*)

Suni's well-traveled foster-home sojourns were the reason I disagreed with having Suni kennel-boarded. I feared Suni would conclude she had been rejected once again. It would be traumatic for the innocent creature and a crying shame since Suni had made first-rate progress in her new home. Credit goes to my daughter, who treats their animals like her children—lots of training, attention, and love.

Suni loved the other dogs! Heck, she loves all living souls! Suni is easily the happiest dog I have ever known. Every ounce of her being is packed with vitality. Her closest playmate is Rico, a sixty-pound Australian Shepherd. Lucy, a 17-pound Cavalier King Charles Spaniel, is quite the lady and though fond of Suni, is not about to relinquish her Queen status.

Now, let us get back to the house-sitting story. My daughter relented. Suni stayed home with Rico and me, but Lucy traveled with my daughter due to her need for timely medication.

I immediately broke Suni of her *'loving'* gesture of clamping her jaws on a person she loves—never hurtful, but naughty nonetheless. My daughter has already corrected that issue, but Suni tried taking advantage of the *'new kid on the block.'* Suni, I suppose, wanted to substitute this gesture for a hug. She arrived with the habit of jumping on people and putting her paws over their shoulders. Ashley broke Suni off this unwelcomed practice, too.

Suni gently clasped her jaws on my clothing when my daughter and son-in-law left. I thumped her on the nose with my thumb as if shooting a marble.

Suni looked surprised, shocked, but attentive. I got right in her face and firmly told her, "Suni, you do not do that when your master is present, and you are not to do that with me or anybody else! Understand! That is a bad, bad 'no-no!' That took care of that.

Previous owners were blind or mistook Suni's intelligence. She learns quickly and patiently endeavors to communicate her desire.

I had placed my house slippers on the floor next to the bed, easy prey for Suni, who took them one at a time to the exercise room. That was Suni's first lesson for me. I placed my slippers on the uppermost part of the exercise machine.

Bewildered, I referred to the list my daughter had left me. Sure enough, item #5 read: "Be careful where you place an item Suni can mistake for a toy. She will take ownership, and it will disappear."

The dogs wanted outside repeatedly, but they also wanted me to accompany them. I decided to save myself the trouble of removing leaves from the dogs' fur coats by blowing the leaves off the back porch and into piles far from the door. The leaf blower would also minimize the dogs' tracking leaves in the house. (*Did I forget to tell you? It was the height of autumn leaves.*)

Once finished, I started weeding the flower beds. Suni supposed I had created the piles of leaves just so she and Rico could play in them. They had a ball!

Suni's tight curly hair was like Velcro for the leaves, requiring brushing! It was funny! Suni looked like a 'walking bush!' Lesson number two, taught by Suni: bag the leaves, or you will need to brush the dogs and rake the leaves again.

While brushing Rico, Suni discovered my weeding tool and played takeaway with me—lesson number three: pick up your tools!

Bedtime came, so I said good night to the dogs and lay on the left side of the king-sized bed. Quickly, Suni leaped onto the bed! I knew Ashley did not allow dogs on the bed. I saw it as another Suni attempt to exploit the '*new kid on the block.*'

I was just about to scold Suni when she reached out with her paw and dragged it across my chest with enough pressure to let me know she was asking me to do something. What was it? They had just come in from their last bathroom break before bed, so it could not be the reason.

I ordered Suni off the bed, and as I did, I moved to the right side of the bed. Now off the bed. Suni looked at me, and I swear she was smiling!

The "*dumb*" dog had taught me yet another lesson: "*The man sleeps on this side of the bed!*"

With great anticipation, I turned off the light and wondered what Suni would teach me tomorrow. Yes, Suni, the dandy Labradoodle, would gladly continue educating me!

TAMARACK, NEW MEXICO

Hear and listen well

For this legend, I will tell

There was a town in New Mexico

It was said, "To Tamarack, do not go."

To avoid it, do your best

Yes, stay away from the southwest

Not if you are inclined to do wrong

Cause in the center of town, tall, strong

Sat the most majestic tree

You ever did see

To Tamarack, do not go

Stay away from New Mexico

Prominent and mighty was the tree

From which wicked ones would dangle free

Maple, ash, sycamore, it was not

Padres prayed for the said tree to rot

If wrongdoing is your thing,

From this tree, you will swing

No, to Tamarack, do not go

Stay away from New Mexico

Solid and healthy was the tree

From it, the evil danced to pay their fee

It was said its beauty and might

Resulted from those who refused to do right

Your death won't be slow

If defying the law is all you know

From this tree, you will swing

Never again to hear the church bell ring

While in Tamarack, do no wrong

Otherwise, your life will not be worth a song

No, to Tamarack, do not go

Stay away from New Mexico

I DON'T DANCE

I don't dance

I don't dance

I don't dance

Allow me to tell you why

The last time I took to the floor,

I wanted to die

First, inform you I must

Vision from one eye is a bust

On the other, blind, I might as well be

I don't dance

I don't dance

I don't dance

All alone in a corner was she

Gallantly, I asked her to dance with me

For her reply, I didn't wait

In my arms, I took her before it was too late

Thin she was and light as a feather

To know her better was my endeavor

I don't dance

I don't dance

I don't dance

You could say she swept me off my feet

Dancing cheek-to-cheek was a treat

A better partner I never had

My heart was pounding, ever so glad

She had the blackest hair, straight as a line

And she followed me ever so fine

In her ear, my words spoke of love

But she was as quiet as a shy dove

I don't dance

I don't dance

I don't dance

The crowd had given us the floor

Laughing, they cheered and applauded

Continually asking for more

The music ended all too soon

Thus, putting a halt to my swoon

I don't dance

I don't dance

I don't dance

From my arms, she was snatched

And, in her corner, she was stashed

OH! NO! NO! NO! MY DOOM! MY DOOM! MY DOOM!

I HAD JUST DANCED WITH A BROOM!!!

Does Anybody Live in Delaware?

Do you know anyone from Delaware?

I know people from everywhere!

Yet, not one single soul from Delaware

I've lived in California, Arkansas, Missouri, Texas, Arizona

But I have never been to Delaware

Does anybody live in Delaware?

I've met people from the Carolinas, Virginias, Dakotas,

And Kansas, but no one from Delaware

News comes from New York, Michigan, Ohio, Tennessee,

Massachusetts, Pennsylvania, and Mississippi

Still, nothing is coming from Delaware

Does anybody live in Delaware?

You hear about Maine, New Mexico, Vermont, Nebraska,

Minnesota, Illinois, New Hampshire, and Louisiana

But what about Delaware?

Does anybody live in Delaware?

Some vacation in Washington, Oregon, Florida, and Alabama

Idaho, Utah, Nevada, Colorado, and Montana

Have yet to hear of someone vacationing in Delaware

Does anybody live in Delaware?

License plates from Connecticut, Kentucky, Indiana,

Wyoming, Maryland, Rhode Island, Iowa, Oklahoma,

But none seen from Delaware

Does anybody live in Delaware?

Have relatives in Georgia, Wisconsin, Hawaii,

Alaska and New Jersey

But no family in Delaware

Does anybody live in Delaware?

People come; people go, I'm aware!

Perhaps, everybody's left Delaware!

Does anybody live in Delaware?

ACE of the DIAMOND

TITO TORRES! OH! What a *béisbol* pitcher was he

Méjico calls the game of baseball *béisbol*; you see

Legend has it his right arm was made of gold

Béisbol knew him only as ACE in letters BOLD

ACE's perfect games/no-hitters enough to spare

When ACE pitched, *Agua Dulce's* losses were rare

In great measure, ACE credited his wife for his success

She charted his every pitch; ACE did loyally confess

Still, no game is more memorable than ACE's last

When ACE faced *Mando Martinez* at his very best

Agua Dulce-Palos Verdes, bitter rivals, were they

Met once each year; September 16th was the day

A year before, *Mando* beat ACE with a two-run blast

Now nineteen, *Mando's* improvement was vast

The Major Leagues dangled *"mucho dinero"* as bait

This game *Mando* must play; the Yankees need wait

Twice *Mando* homered and should have had a third

But he failed in touching them all, running too hard

In the ninth, ACE willed for an inning of 1, 2, three

But NO! An E-5! From *Mando,* ACE was not yet free

Here is the setting: tying run on second and two out

The fans rose when ACE's catcher called time out

ACE's fans wanted *Mando* to walk intentionally

ACE shook his head; his pride would not agree

Thirteen pitches came *Mando's* way; all but three

Mando's bat scattered like missiles; FOUL, thankfully

Jubilant fans witnessed a classic confrontation

Standing still, they cheered every foul in admiration

Before his last pitch, ACE stood tall on the mound

In the dugout, ACE's wife could hear her heart pound

ACE now turned and rocked, his arms swinging at his side

He pivoted his body, and his left leg took a perfect stride

Pitch selection and location made *Mando* swing a tad late

Mando grinned and tipped his cap to ACE, accepting his fate

Proudly, ACE removed his cap, thus returning the flattery

And left the mound for the last time and joined his family

ABOUT THE AUTHOR

Born in Mexico did not dissuade Rosalío *'Ross'* Sánchez' goal of striving to be a grade-school teacher/coach.

While living in a rural, pastoral area of Brownsville, Texas, Gregorio and María instilled a hard-work ethic in their youngsters.

As a pre-teen, the author's parents moved the family to California. Ross' teachers and coaches strengthened his dream to teach and coach.

After achieving his teaching degree from Fresno State, Ross enjoyed an esteemed thirty-three-year career. As a teacher, Mr. Sánchez effectively narrated his and others' experiences to his students as learning lessons.

Upon retirement, Ross and his second daughter, Valery, joined Ashley, the first-born daughter, in northwest Arkansas. Here, the beauty of the area motivated his writing.

Ross' closeness with his daughters provides comfort and support, plus encouragement.

This book is dedicated to TODD BOWEN for the idea the youngster gave his teacher.

Made in the USA
Las Vegas, NV
21 September 2023

77843506R00142